and the DEADHEADS

MILLTOWN N.S
RATHCONRATH
MULLINGAR

THE HAUNTING

Roy Apps

MACDONALD YOUNG BOOKS

To Peter Hoare

First published in 1996 by
Andersen Press Limited

This edition published in 1997 by
Macdonald Young Books,
an imprint of Wayland Publishers
61 Western Road
Hove
BN3 1JD

Text © Roy Apps 1996

British Library Cataloguing in Publication Data is available.

ISBN 0 7500 2183 7

Phototypeset by Intype London Ltd
Printed and bound in Great Britain by
The Guernsey Press Co Ltd

Cover illustration © Paul Young 1996

Melvin
and the DEADHEADS

I

Esther's ginger moustache bristles with excitement. As Head Teacher of Sir Norman Burke Middle School it is his job to raise as much money as possible for things like science equipment and textbooks. The summer term has started well. The Chief Executive of WhoppaShoppa UK has just paid him handsomely to use the school hall for a public meeting.

Esther leads the sharp-suited businessman down the corridor past the Art Room where rows of papier mâché monster masks, all bearing ginger moustaches, beam menacingly at them.

'The conditions are: no alcohol, nothing that is likely to result in a breach of the peace and definitely no chewing gum,' says Esther severely: for being a Head Teacher, he just can't get out of the habit of telling people the school rules.

'Understood, Mr Ranson,' says the Chief Executive of WhoppaShoppa UK, his ingratiating voice as oily as a can of sardines. 'But the purpose of our meeting is simply to allow the people of Smallham to air their concerns about our proposed shopping mall development.'

'Everyone in Smallham is against it,' warns Esther.

'I'm certain that once we have reassured them, they'll soon be changing their minds,' replies the Chief Executive of WhoppaShoppa in a tone that Esther finds threatening, rather than reassuring.

The two men come to the end of the corridor.

'This is the school hall,' says Esther, pushing open the double doors. The raucous din of two hundred Middle School pupils stuffing their faces with plates of school dinner, cans of Coke and packets of crisps assaults the men's ears.

Suddenly, above this cacophony, there shrieks a clear and threatening voice: 'Oi! Perkins! Fetch us the ketchup!'

Esther winces; pulls the Chief Executive of WhoppaShoppa UK out of the hall and quickly closes the doors. He hurries his guest away to where his black BMW lies waiting in the teachers' car park.

'Ah ... very high-spirited some of our young charges are,' says Esther, his thin smile unable to hide his embarrassment completely.

The Chief Executive of WhoppaShoppa UK grunts disdainfully, as if to say that if such undisciplined yobbos ever dared cross his path, they would soon lose their 'high spirits'.

Which goes to show just how wrong you can be.

1

7GG's P.W.S.T.

'Oi! Perkins! Fetch us the ketchup!'

A few sharp-eyed diners noticed their Head Teacher usher his guest out of the double doors as the clear and threatening voice rose above all others in the school hall. They couldn't blame him. After all, the voice belonged to 7GG's P.W.S.T.

I shall explain.

Most classes have two or three P.W.S.T.s; that is, *Persons What Spell Trouble*. You know the sort of people I mean. The ones you try and make sure you're never sitting next to in class. The ones you always keep half an anxious eye out for in the playground, in the same way you might keep an eye out for killer aliens after you've been watching your dad's video of *The X-Files*.

Mr Gibbons' class – 7GG – only had the *one* P.W.S.T. But 7GG's P.W.S.T. was a *Person What Spelt Trouble* like no other. 7GG's P.W.S.T. swopped the disk in the music room computer with a disk of rugby songs which were all about the rude bits of your body. 7GG's P.W.S.T. wrote a note and slipped it into the class register. It was signed 'Carol Higgins (Mrs)'. It asked if her darling son Damien (captain of the football team) could transfer from football to Country Dancing as this would help his plans to become a ballroom dancer when he left school. 7GG's P.W.S.T. strutted around Sir Norman Burke Middle School in size seven DMs and bawled at you like a Gestapo officer.

7GG's P.W.S.T. was called Cassandra Washbone.

'Oi! Perkins!' she yelled at Melvin Perkins, for the second time of asking.

She was at the top end of the hall by the stage, surrounded by her henchwomen, screeching, cackling and munching her way through a cheeseburger. Melvin was at the other end of the hall, by the kitchen hatch, sharing a rhubarb yoghurt with Pravikumar Patel. When Cassandra Washbone spoke to – or rather yelled at – you, there wasn't much point pretending you hadn't heard. Slowly, Melvin raised his eyes from his lunchbox.

'Fetch us the ketchup!' boomed Cassandra.

Pravikumar looked anxiously at Melvin and quickly tried to hunch himself up into his blazer like a tortoise disappearing into his shell: he was afraid he was next in line for the P.W.S.T. treatment. Melvin looked around. The only dinner supervisor was busy mopping up a puddle of sick from under one of the Year 4 tables. There wasn't a teacher in sight. Well, you know what teachers are like. They all scamper off to the staff room at lunch time and barricade themselves in until the bell goes. The teachers at Sir Norman Burke Middle School were no different from any others.

'You heard me, Perkins! Fetch us the ketchup or else . . .!'

Melvin dearly wanted to say, 'Or else what?' But he daren't.

'I shall sit next to you in French!'

Two hundred jaws stopped chomping and started dropping. Sandwiches, crisps, cans of Coke all seemed to be frozen in mid-air. Then four hundred eyes turned to look at Melvin, to see whether he would take Cassandra Washbone the ketchup or tell her where to go.

It was no contest. Sitting next to Cassandra Washbone in French would've meant having to have conversations with her about the colour of *votre bicyclette* and the job of *votre père*. As he didn't know the French for fluorescent turquoise with purple stripes and as his dad had left home just after his little sister was born, Melvin reckoned that French was a time when it was well smart to sit as far away from Cassandra Washbone as possible.

So he got up, grabbed the ketchup from the kitchen hatch, and made his way over to her. Cassandra's sneer could've curdled a pot of cream at a hundred paces.

'Good boy, Lassie,' she smirked. 'Only next time, be a bit more sharpish about it.'

Cassandra had nicknamed Melvin 'Lassie'. '*He's*

like a flippin' dog. He does everything I tell him. And he does everything the teachers tell him.' Which wasn't strictly true. It was simply that Melvin tried to observe Perkins' First Law of Survival which stated: Keep Your Head Down. You see, Melvin was *average-ish* at most things and well, he reckoned he preferred it that way. As he had once explained to Pravikumar while they huddled round a freezing goalpost during a mid-winter games lesson:

'Once you start showing any signs of being good at anything the teachers are down on you like a ton of bricks – "Have you thought about joining the school choir . . .? Would you like a game in the first eleven . . .?" I just want to get on with my own life. And I wish other people would do the same with theirs.'

Now where was I? Oh yes, the school hall . . .

'Hang on a minute, Lassie!'

Cassandra pointed to the ketchup bottle on the table.

'I've done with it now, thank you. You can take it back.'

Melvin turned, walked back and quickly picked up the bottle. Immediately, two hundred gleeful guffaws filled his ears as ketchup dripped all the way down his hand and up the sleeve of his jumper. P.W.S.T. that she was, Cassandra had taken the trouble to smear dollops of the stuff all round

10

the outside of the bottle.

Melvin tried to act tough walking back, willing himself to be like Clint Eastwood, but the more he tried to hold his head up, the more he kept tripping over people's bags.

By the time he sat down, his hand and cuff were still dripping ketchup. He looked as if he had just put his arm into a tankful of man-eating piranha fish.

Pravikumar made a face that said 'Urgh!'

'Don't worry about it, Pravi. Just something I've got up my sleeve,' mumbled Melvin. The more he wiped it up with his hankie, the more it got everywhere. Pravi peered over his glasses and saw that Melvin's eyes were all watery.

'Melv ... ' said Pravi.

'What?'

'You can borrow this over the weekend if you like.' Pravi held out a thick paperback book with a bright shiny cover.

The Giant Vole of Gordian was the sixteenth and latest book in *The Lay of the Dork* series. Pravi's dad ran a big newsagent's and he always got the new titles as soon as they'd come out. It was the big thing Pravi and Melvin had in common, *The Lay of the Dork* books. They were both big fans. In fact, if the truth be known, it was probably the *only* thing they had in common. Melvin didn't know a lot about Pravi really, and Pravi didn't know much about Melvin.

'Ta,' Melvin said.

''Salright,' shrugged Pravi.

But Melvin's mind was still on Cassandra Wash-bone. 'One of these days, I'll show her!' he muttered darkly.

'Show her what?' asked Pravi innocently.

'Teach her a thing or two!'

'Oh.' Pravi sighed wearily, like someone who had heard it all before. There was a good reason for this. He had.

'I mean it,' said Melvin, unconvincingly. But deep down he knew he was just kidding himself. Deep down he knew he was going to stick to Perkins' First Law of Survival (Keep Your Head Down) for the rest of his life. At the least for the rest of his life at Sir Norman Burke Middle School.

Which goes to show just how wrong you can be.

II

The Chief Executive of WhoppaShoppa UK's mobile phone trills out a flat little tune as its owner's fat fingers punch out a familiar series of digits.

'Darius? Harry. It's all sorted. I paid the school well over the odds. That pleased 'em. It should be worth it. Guy was right. The hall's massive. We'll be able to pack 'em in.'

'They didn't seem suspicious?'

'Suspicious? Why should they be? They think it's just a public relations meeting about a new shopping mall.' He chuckles long and loud to himself, a chuckle chilling enough to raise goosebumps on your arms. Even on a summer's night as warm as this one.

2

'Gone to the end of the Universe. Will maintain radio contact . . .'

Melvin lay on his bed and studied the cover of *The Lay of the Dork: The Sixteenth Saga: The Giant Vole of Gordian*. Murphin the Grule was effecting a bloody revenge on a Gordian Vole with his trusty witchhazel stave. Melvin was looking forward to the read. He was hoping it might offer some tips as to how he could wreak a dreadful revenge on Cassandra Washbone. Someone or something was always wreaking terrible revenge in *The Lay of the Dork* books. Melvin didn't even have time to open *The Giant Vole of Gordian* before he heard shrill voices coming through his bedroom wall.

'Go and stay at your frigging mother's then!'

'All right, I will!'

'Good.'

'Don't think you'll get the car.'

'That's all you think about. Your car.'

'I'm not saying nothing else. You'll have to speak to my sister.'

'Slister!'

'What?'

'It's slister. Not sister! Stupid.'

'No it's not . . .!'

14

Melvin's five-year-old sister Ellie and her friend were playing Families again. They believed in playing realistically. Melvin pushed his fingers into his ears to try and drown out the sounds of the two girls acting out scenes of domestic violence. It was no use, of course. Try it sometime: you'll find there's no way you can hold a book when you've got your fingers in your ears.

Melvin sighed, picked up *The Giant Vole of Gordian* and made his way downstairs to the sitting room. No sooner had he got his hand on the door handle than a piercing scream filled the air.

'Aaargh!!! E-e-e-arghhhh! E-e-e-arghhhh!'

Melvin didn't flinch. Even though he recognised the dreadful screams as coming from his mum, he let his hand drop from the door handle. He knew exactly what was causing his mum to scream like that: it was Zho'neng-Do.

Now, you're probably thinking that Zho'neng-Do was Melvin's evil stepfather or the family's sadistic lodger – but you're wrong. Zho'neng-Do was Melvin's mum's latest craze. Zho'neng-Do involved a lot of arm and leg waving and even more yelling and screaming.

'No, Melvin, it is not "barmy nonsense",' his mum had told him when she had first started doing Zho'neng-Do exercises. 'It's an ancient oriental martial art that leads to an extraordinary inner peace.'

15

'It might provide you with an extraordinary inner peace,' Melvin had told her, 'but it provides me with an extraordinary inner headache.'

That had been four weeks ago, just before the beginning of the summer term. Since then, stories about plans to build a shopping-centre on Hogman's Meadow had appeared in the *Smallham Gazette* and at a packed meeting, Melvin's mum had been elected secretary of the SSNOTS! ('Smallham Says NO to Shopping-centre') campaign. Melvin had hoped that this new interest would result in her Zho'neng-Do exercises resting in everlasting inner peace, but she showed no sign of wavering in her enthusiasm for the ancient martial art.

Melvin sighed again, made his way through to the kitchen, sat down at the table and opened *The Giant Vole of Gordian* at page one. The spine crackled enticingly.

BOOM-OOM-OOM THUD! BOOM-OOM-OOM THUD!

The cracks in the kitchen ceiling opened and closed in time with the heavy bass rhythm pounding out above. Melvin's older sister Hannah was playing her house music; and house music, as you know, is called house music because it has to be played so loud that everyone in the *house* can hear it.

Once more, Melvin sighed. He needed peace and quiet to read *The Giant Vole of Gordian* and he wasn't going to get it at home. He got up and scribbled 'GONE TO THE END OF THE UNIVERSE. WILL MAINTAIN RADIO CONTACT. M' on the notice board above the fridge. Then he slipped out of the back door, hauled his bike out of the shed and then wondered just where he should go.

You see, when the Saxons or whoever gave Smallham its name, they were spot on. Smallham was – and always had been – a *small* town. There were two schools (First and Middle), four pubs, a few shops, a recreation ground known as the 'rec' because that's what it was – a *wreck* – and a Chinese takeaway that sold fish and chips. It was twelve miles from civilisation – i.e. the MGM Multi-screen & Leisure Centre, and five miles as the sea-gull flies, over the South Downs to the sea.

There were only three roads out of Smallham. Station Road led down to one end of the bypass; North Street up to the other. Before they built the bypass along the course of the old railway, traffic hurtled at breakneck speed along the High Street in a desperate rush to get through the place and out the other side as soon as possible.

The third road, Hogman's Hill, rose steeply past Hogman's Meadow, Hogman's Thorn House and up and on through the large, sprawling wood known as Hogman's Thorn before eventually fanning out into a series of chalky car parks on top of the wind-swept Downs.

Melvin knew he had no choice. Standing high off

the saddle and pushing hard on the pedals, he headed up Hogman's Hill, his bike swinging recklessly beneath him.

III

The village is no more than a farmhouse, a few cottages and a disused church. The lane winding up to it leads nowhere else, making it isolated and difficult to reach. That is the way they like it. That is the way they need it.

There are four of them: three men and a woman. They sit around the gnarled farmhouse table, their faces all filled with the same crushing hardness.

A thick-set young man in security guard's uniform knocks and enters the kitchen.

'Get over to the house and open up,' orders one of the men; whom the Head Teacher of Sir Norman Burke Middle School would have recognised instantly as the Chief Executive of WhoppaShoppa UK. 'Take the dog. Check the grounds.'

'Yes, Mr Summerskill.'

'Are you expecting trouble, Harry?' asks the woman.

'No. Just being careful, Angela, As always.'

Through the lattice window the guard can be seen dragging a snarling Dobermann pinscher into the back of a van. The van rocks from side to side as the dog throws itself against the locked doors.

The youngest of the three men, dressed in a charcoal grey suit that is as sharp as a razor, turns away from the window to the Chief Executive of Whoppa-Shoppa UK. 'Is he safe?'

'The dog?'

'The thug who's handling the dog.'

'Of course he's safe, Darius. Look at his eyes. No sign of life in them. I topped him up last night. He's a deadhead all right.'

'For how long?' asks the third man.

The Chief Executive of WhoppaShoppa UK's coarse and self-confident laugh carries no trace of humour. 'For ever, Guy. For ever.'

3

'HO HO HO it said . . .'

The further up Hogman's Hill you went, the bigger the houses got. They started as terraced cottages, grew into numbered semis and finally blossomed into detached houses with names like 'Pippins' and 'Conifers'. On that bright summer's morning when Melvin pedalled past them, they all sported bright yellow posters in their front windows declaring, 'I'M FOR SSNOTS!'

Melvin pumped the pedals of his bike up and down furiously, keen to keep up a steady rhythm. Hogman's Hill was steep, long and winding – hardly ideal cycling terrain. But it was the only way out of Smallham, if you were on a bike.

Melvin enjoyed cycling up it though, particularly the way it made his blood pound noisily through his head, shutting out all the sounds of the outside world. His head was down over the handlebars. He was nearing the top of the hill, where the road ran parallel with a long, high brick wall. This wall marked the boundary of Hogman's Thorn House and buckled and bent like a boxer on his last legs. He looked up and noticed with some surprise that the huge wrought iron gates in the wall were open.

When he had last ridden by, they had been chained up, as they had been ever since the old lady who had lived in the house had died months ago.

Melvin stopped. He needed to get his breath back. He pushed his bike in through the gates. Only just mind: Perkins' First Law of Survival (Keep Your Head Down) sang a warning song through his head.

Heavy tyre treads had worn a path through the thick carpet of moss and weeds that covered the drive. Gangly trees, shrubs and bushes, heavy with leaves, towered over the whole place, making it seem more like a tropical rain forest than a country garden. Melvin could just make out the lines of the house itself, a couple of hundred metres or so away. Gables stuck out of the roof as if the builder had just decided to plonk them there any old how. Layers of scaffolding rose against the side wall. Melvin grinned. He imagined his mum looking around and saying:

'Melvin this place looks like a bomb has hit it! I want to see it tidied up and some semblance of order restored before I get back from the shops. Are you listening to me, Melvin?'

Hogman's Thorn House might have been only a half mile or so out of the town, but it seemed to Melvin as if he had arrived in another world. Hogman's Meadow, on which WhoppaShoppa planned to build their shopping-centre, lay between the grounds and the last house in Smallham proper, and on two other sides the house was surrounded by the dense woods of Hogman's Thorn.

A sudden creak sent an uncomfortable tingle down Melvin's spine. Instinctively, he dropped his bike and spun round. Nothing. Just a huge board he had not noticed before, swinging gently on a rusting chain above the outside wall.

HO HO HO

it said. Melvin found himself shivering involuntarily. He didn't like its tone. Even though he pretty quickly worked out that some witty wally had simply removed most of the letters from the old sign saying 'HOGMAN'S THORN HOUSE', it seemed to be mocking him. Perkins' First Law of Survival (Keep Your Head Down) flashed its bright warning light across his mind again. He wanted out.

Quickly, he turned back round to pick up his bike. And froze. About four metres away stood a boy. About his age, Melvin guessed. About to ask him why he was trespassing, Melvin guessed. About to give him a thump, Melvin guessed.

'Er . . . sorry. Got lost,' he stuttered.

The boy took a few steps towards him. He didn't recognise him as a Norman Burke type. He was scruffy. His trousers were ripped right up to the knee, his shirt didn't have a collar and his filthy hair resembled a mophead.

'Do you see me?' he asked Melvin. 'Do you hear me?'

Even though the boy spoke quietly, it sounded to Melvin like a threat. 'Yeah . . . all right, I heard you. I said. Got lost. I'm just going . . .' He pulled his bike towards the gateway. The boy followed.

'Topper machine.'

The boy was staring at Melvin's bike like it was an alien spacecraft. Melvin decided he was a Fruit Cake.

'What are you staring at? Haven't you ever seen a bike before?'

Fruit Cake stood there, shifting his stare from Melvin's bike to his face. 'You can't go!' It was almost a plea.

'Can't I? Just watch me!' Melvin pedalled out of the gate and turned to look up Hogman's Hill toward the Thorn to check that the road was clear.

It wasn't.

There were three figures on the other side of the road, roller-blading down the footpath into Smallham. Three figures Melvin recognised immediately: Cassandra Washbone and her cronies Jodie Jenkins and Kayleigh Foster. As they were yelling their heads off at each other they hadn't seen Melvin, but he knew if he didn't get out of the drive and down Hogman's Hill quickly, they soon would. The sneering tones of 7GG's P.W.S.T. was the last thing Melvin wanted to face on a sunny summer

Saturday morning.

A glance down the hill told Melvin there were two cars he would need to let go by before he could get out onto the road. And that was two cars too many. There was nothing else for it. Melvin back-tracked into the drive, leapt off his bike and began dragging it out of sight of the gateway up against the inside of the wall.

Shrubs and bushes had grown close up to the wall and it was hard work pushing through them. The ground was moist and springy, but littered with crisp packets and sweet wrappings, blown over the wall from the windows of passing cars and lorries. Most of the bushes were taller than Melvin, and thin shafts of coloured sunlight filtered down through the dark green leaves.

Fruit Cake seemed to appear at Melvin's shoulder instantly.

'Very few people come here and see me,' he breathed in Melvin's ear.

'I haven't come to see you,' Melvin said, tetchily. 'I've come to stop *them* seeing *me!*'

Already he could hear the Washbone's foghorn voice above the grinding clatter of three pairs of roller-blades.

'They are enemies of yours?' asked Fruit Cake.

'You could say that,' Melvin muttered.

'Have they done you some great harm?'

'For crying out loud, shut up – and keep out

25

of sight!'

But Fruit Cake had already gone to the gate. He stood there looking up the road. There seemed to be no way that the Washbone and her henchwomen could avoid seeing him.

'Get back here!'

He dashed back. 'They've crossed over the lane, I warrant they're heading this way!'

'What!' Melvin dragged his bike down with him behind a large bush – and winced. It was a prickly bush. 'Careful!' he hissed as the boy threw himself down beside him. 'It's a rose or something.' But Fruit Cake didn't appear to be bothered by a few vicious rose thorns. Perhaps being mad means you're naturally hard, thought Melvin.

The Washbone's voice was quite clear now. 'Yeah, well I'm right, see!'

As if anyone would ever doubt it.

'Bunny told me.'

'Your brother? What does he know?' Jodie asked sarcastically.

'He's at College, isn't he?'

'So?'

'So he's studying Photography and Video and that and he said the guy who services all their equipment had been here installing all the latest editing and dubbing gear. It's obvious, isn't it? They'll be making promos, rock videos, adverts, the lot. I'm going to get a slice of the action.'

'You're what?'

'Get some interviews with actors, rock stars and that. It'll stand me in good stead.'

'For what?'

'For getting a job as a telly presenter when I leave school – or college.'

Melvin shuddered. The Washbone's leering grin being beamed into twenty million homes across the country was a terrifying thought indeed.

'And there's really a film studio in there . . .?' Kayleigh sounded doubtful.

'Yeah! Come on! I'll show you!'

'I'm not roller-blading up this filthy dirt track,' protested Jodie.

'Nor am I,' said Kayleigh.

'Oh . . . all right,' growled Cassandra, who obviously didn't fancy roller-blading along inch deep lorry ruts either. Her voice drifted off out of the grounds and down the hill. Melvin closed his eyes with relief.

When he opened them, Fruit Cake was still staring at him.

'Thanks for warning me,' Melvin said, rather grudgingly.

Fruit Cake shrugged.

'Lucky they didn't see you,' Melvin added.

'You're lucky that you can,' replied Fruit Cake quickly.

This guy is well freaky, Melvin thought. But somehow he didn't feel uneasy with him. The boy's eyes, as he stared at Melvin, were very pale. They seemed to Melvin to have a kind of sad and lost look. Being stared at by him wasn't like being eye-balled by the Washbone.

'Where are you from then?' Melvin asked him.

'Brighton.'

'Brighton? That's miles away! What are you doing up here?'

'I live here.'

Melvin didn't believe him. 'I've never seen you in Smallham.'

'You've seen me now.'

'Where do you go to school?'

'I live *here*.' The boy nodded in the direction of HO HO HO.

'Is your dad working here or something then?'

Fruit Cake shook his head. 'I have no father.'

'Oh. Right . . .' Melvin wished then that he hadn't opened his big mouth. He knew how sick he still felt when people asked him about his dad: always a bit of him wanted to lie and say he worked on an oil rig or something, while another bit of him wanted to cry and yet another bit of him wanted to knock their teeth down their throat for making him think about his dad. Fruit Cake didn't look upset though.

'My dad walked out. Just after my sister was

born,' Melvin found himself saying. And it wasn't until he had said it that he realised he had never told anybody before. But here, in this other world of an overgrown garden, with a Fruit Cake who also had no father, it somehow seemed the natural thing to do.

'Does your mother have means?' asked Fruit Cake.

'*Means*?'

'You haven't been forced upon the mercies of the guardians?'

'Eh...? Oh! No, I don't live with a guardian. I live with my mum – and sisters. My mum's a teacher.'

Melvin was sure he saw Fruit Cake shudder.

'If you live here, who looks after you?'

'I am quite alone.'

'You live *alone*?' Melvin didn't believe him. He couldn't believe him.

'My aunt sent me here. I fancy I was a source of trouble – and expense – to her.'

Before Melvin could ask him anything else, Fruit Cake had leapt up and started moving towards the house.

'Tell me, what do they call you?'

'Melvin Perkins.'

'I'm Thomas – christened, yes christened I was – with the name of Arnold. Come along!'

Arnold moved off towards the house. Melvin

pulled his bike from the bushes, leapt on to the saddle and rode after him. The drive twisted and turned, but eventually opened onto a large sweeping frontage, which Melvin was surprised to see had been smartly laid with tarmac. There was a heap of dark yellow sand and a small pile of bricks, but it was obvious that much rebuilding work had already been carried out on the house. The spruced up red brickwork glowed in the summer morning sunlight. But despite this, the same sunlight somehow made the building look cold and disconcerting. When he moved closer, Melvin realised why: the sunlight was not being reflected in any of the windows. They were all opaque, like the windows of a customised car. The Washbone was right after all, thought Melvin, they have built a studio inside.

'Halloa!' called Arnold. 'This way, Perkins!' He disappeared round the far side of the house. Melvin dropped his bike to join him.

He was at the corner of the house when he heard the squeal of brakes.

Melvin spun round and saw that a van had come to rest inches from his sprawling bike. The uniformed driver had spotted him and was already striding his way across, in the company of an enormous, ugly-looking guard dog, which Melvin recognised as a Dobermann pinscher.

'You've got two minutes, punk, then I take the

choke off Lassie here,' snarled the security guard.

'I was invited up here,' began Melvin.

The dog began to pant and strain on its leash.

' – By Arnold . . . Arnold Thomas . . . he lives here . . .?'

'Don't mess with me. No one lives here.' The guard's eyes were as hard as a pair of buttons. They were fixed unwaveringly on Melvin's face.

'But . . .' Melvin picked up his bike and saw Arnold standing a few feet behind the driver and his dog. 'There he is! Arnold!'

The guard glanced round, but appeared to see nothing.

'Aargh!'

Suddenly Melvin's arm was locked into the security guard's fist and pushed to within a few centimetres of the dog's slavering jaws. Melvin could feel the animal's stale, steamy breath on his skin.

'You ever seen a face that's been mauled by a dog?'

'Ow . . .! Er . . . n-no!'

'Look at a plate of liver in the butcher's window. You'll get the picture.' The guard released Melvin's arm. 'Thirty seconds!'

Melvin leapt onto his bike and sped back down the drive without daring to look back. Even when he reached the gates, he could still hear the dog snarling excitedly. Melvin felt sick to the pit of

31

his stomach.

He had good reason to.

For the gates of HO HO HO were locked fast.

Melvin swore; kicked the gates; swore some more. His hands and armpits were sticky with sweat. His thirty seconds were up; he knew that. He was sure the sound of the snarling dog was getting closer. He looked round. Arnold stood in the drive. He showed no sign of fear whatsoever.

'Make haste! Wheel your machine into the shrubbery!'

'Thanks for backing me up, scumbag,' muttered Melvin, squeezing himself and his bike between the wall and the thick, claw-like branches of the bushes. The barking was becoming more excited; and it was getting closer.

'Now if you stand on the seat of your machine you ought to be able to reach the top of the wall with your hands,' advised Arnold calmly.

'What else did you think I was going to do, stupid?' retorted Melvin, though in truth he'd had no idea. He leant his bike against the wall, heaved himself up onto the saddle and, grabbing the top of the wall with both hands, inched his way up, until he was lying on the top.

'Are you coming?' Melvin called to Arnold.

'I can't.'

'You're barmy! What about the dog?' Melvin could hear the dog sniffing and growling its way along the wall from the drive.

'He can't harm me.'

Melvin knew he had no time to argue further. He put his arm down to haul up his bike, but found that his fingers only just scraped the saddle: there was no way, without risk of falling off the wall, that he could get a grip on it. 'Pass me my bike up then!'

Arnold shook his head. 'I am sorry, Perkins, but that is something I cannot do.'

'Of course you can! Just pick it up so that I can grab hold of the crossbar!'

'I would if I could, I swear to you.'

Melvin called Arnold a lot of rude names, most of which began with 'b'. 'Don't go thinking you can nick it. It's post coded!'

'Perkins old chap, trust me. I assure you, I will guard your machine until your return!'

Melvin shook his head, swung his legs over the wall and dropped down onto the narrow grass verge at the side of Hogman's Hill. The midday sun seemed suddenly bright and he screwed his eyes against the light.

'You look after that bike, or else I get the police. Right?' he called through the wall.

There was no reply.

'I mean it!' Melvin threatened.

There was still no reply from Arnold. Melvin could hear the dog though; it wasn't snarling or growling but whimpering like a puppy.

Melvin turned on his heels and began to walk down Hogman's Hill towards Smallham, too frightened, too angry and too hungry to wonder why.

IV

The large black BMW speeds up Hogman's Hill. The driver turns to the young woman in the front passenger seat.

'Read what it says in The Gazette, Angela.'

The woman turns to the main story on the front page. 'The might and money of a large commercial corporation can be thwarted. We urge every resident of Smallham to attend the public meeting on Monday and make their views known,' she reads.

'I do love free advertising, Angela.'

'It seems you were right, Harry. They have fallen for it in a big way, haven't they?'

'Of course they have!' The Chief Executive of WhoppaShoppa UK sounds supremely self-confident. 'And why not? What do they know of the real agenda?'

He peers through the windscreen at the tidy cottage gardens.

'For them, poor benighted souls, deadheading is merely something you do to your roses...'

His lips spread out into a humourless grin.

4

'Yes, Mum. No, Mum. Sorry, Mum.'

'You're late!'

'Sorry, Mum. I had to walk back.'

'Where's your bike then?'

'Er . . . I left it with a friend.'

'Pravi?'

'Er . . . no . . .'

'Who then?'

'Someone . . . er . . . no one you know.'

'Melvin . . .!'

'It's safe, Mum.' Melvin wished he believed what he was saying.

'If you get this one stolen too, you're not getting another. It's not insured, you know. And look at you! You look as if you've been dragged through a hedge backwards!'

I have, thought Melvin.

Melvin's mum fluttered her eyelids and pouted into her compact mirror, then snapped it shut and stuffed it into an overflowing shoulder bag.

'What have you been doing?'

Melvin judged that any attempt to explain his encounter with a Fruit Cake, a psychopathic security guard and a slavering Dobermann pinscher would probably not improve his mum's mood. She brushed by him on her way to the hall.

'You knew I wanted you back for an early lunch!'

'Er...'

'I told you at breakfast!'

Perkins' Second Law of Survival was: Never Listen To Anything Anyone Says At Breakfast.

Melvin's mum appeared from the cupboard under the stairs clutching a pair of shoes. 'I've got a SSNOTS committee this afternoon. It's the big public meeting up at the school Monday night and we've got to have our case thoroughly prepared.'

'Yes, Mum.'

'We know that a major natural habitat of the stone curlew and the wart-biter cricket will be destroyed, but what do we know of the wart-biter itself?'

'It bites warts?' suggested Melvin.

His mum ignored him. 'And of course the WhoppaShoppa will mean more traffic and lorries trundling through the town centre, but we need to know *how* much more.'

'Yes, Mum.'

'WhoppaShoppa UK will have barristers, public relations guys and goodness knows who else on their side. All we've got on our side are the people of Smallham – and right, of course.'

'Yes, Mum.' Melvin clapped his hands politely.

'Councillor Washbone's already agreed to chair

Monday's meeting.'

'I thought the council had approved the Whoppa-Shoppa development?'

Melvin's mum sighed. 'That was the *county* council, Melvin, not the *town* council. Don't you listen to anything I explain to you? There's houmous and pitta bread in the fridge.'

'Yes, Mum.'

Melvin's mum pulled on her shoes and hitched up her skirt. 'And stay here with Ellie until I get back. She's playing in her room at the moment.'

'Can't Hannah look after her?'

'Hannah's gone to see a friend.'

'What friend?'

'I'll only be a couple of hours.'

'What about my bike?'

But the front door had already slammed shut.

What about my bike? thought Melvin. I'll need a rope and I'll need help. I'm not going back there on my own.

Melvin knew that the only person who might lend him a hand was Pravi Patel and he wasn't going to be around until after school on Monday.

He sighed, scooped a few dollops of houmous into some pitta bread, put his feet up on the kitchen table and pulled out *The Giant Vole of Gordian* from his jacket pocket.

'Melvin, can I go and play with Kate?' A bored Ellie appeared at the kitchen door.

'No.'

'Why not?'

'Because you've got to stay here.'

'You're a . . . you're a *hoolinagism*!' bawled Ellie, stomping back to her room.

Melvin sighed. He opened *The Giant Vole of Gordian* and began to read:

Murphin the Grule, sage of the Brummis, peered deep into his crystal goblet. 'Beware the tribe of Gordian Voles . . .'

Melvin's eyes moved across the words on the first page, but he found he wasn't reading them. It was as if they were in a strange language that meant nothing to him. Burrowing their way through his mind were constant images of slavering dogs and tattooed security guards. He shivered. If only the Washbone hadn't appeared when she had, he could have ridden out of the grounds of HO HO HO. His bike would be in the back yard now instead of with that pale-faced Fruit Cake, Arnold.

He tried to make sense of Arnold's story, hoping it might make the thought of having to go back to the HO HO HO less dreadful. Obviously all that stuff about his aunt sending him there to live alone was a huge wind-up – or just part of being a Fruit Cake. No, Melvin reckoned, Arnold's dad was the caretaker and they lived in a flat round the back of the house. That would explain why he had never seen him at school; they would have only just moved in. And judging from Arnold's weird way of talking, they probably used to live in Cornwall or Wales where people have peculiar accents. Yes, it all added up. No doubt Arnold was friendly with the dog, feeding it steak and kidney: yes, that was why he'd said it wouldn't harm him.

But Arnold hadn't said that!

Melvin could hear his strange, reedy voice even now:

'*He* can't *harm me.*'

Melvin felt his lips going dry. Suddenly, his comforting explanation of Arnold began to unravel alarmingly. Why had the security guard told him that nobody lived at HO HO HO? Why hadn't *he* seen Arnold? Why hadn't Arnold helped him with his bike? Why had that brute of a dog been whimpering when he climbed over the wall? With an effort, Melvin swallowed a mouthful of food. He got up and tipped the rest into the bin.

He didn't feel hungry any more.

V

The burly young security guard coaxes the whimpering Dobermann pinscher back onto its leash. He is frightened. He has never seen the animal like this before. It's a wild, half-mad creature, for heaven's sake – a guard dog.

A big, black BMW swerves into the drive.

He ought to tell Mr Summerskill, he knows. He has to tell Mr Summerskill everything. He starts to walk up the drive, rehearsing what he might say. Then it occurs to him that Mr Summerskill will want to know how a boy on a bike had got into the grounds in the first place and he will have to say that he had forgotten to lock the gates the previous evening. And Mr Summerskill will be angry. The guard doesn't like it when Mr Summerskill is angry.

He thinks to himself, perhaps I won't tell Mr Summerskill this time. After all, it was only a scrawny kid nosing around. Nobody dangerous.

5

'We're going to beat them, Melvin . . .!'

'Who cares about wart-biters?' boomed Cassandra Washbone. 'Grisly, primitive creatures.'

'Speak for yourself!' muttered Damien Higgins.

'Thank you, Damien,' Mr Gibbons said, 'let Cassandra present her argument.'

Mr Gibbons had arranged for 7GG to spend the entire Monday afternoon staging their own version of that evening's Public Debate on the proposed development of Hogman's Meadow. Nearly all were against it: they sensed instinctively that the loss of an important natural habitat would somehow be a *bad thing* not just for the wart-biter cricket that lived in Hogman's Meadow, but for the whole of Smallham.

Pravi Patel and Bomber Bromley, whose dad ran the butcher's shop, explained how their parents could go out of business.

Sarah Jupe quietly pointed out that the Whoppa-Shoppa would mean heavy lorries trundling up and down the High Street. There was an uneasy silence when she finished speaking: everyone knew that her little brother had died under the wheels of a juggernaut just a few weeks before the bypass

42

had opened.

Only a few children from outlying villages and farms were undecided and only Cassandra Washbone was *for* the proposed development.

'As for the wonderful new shopping-centre destroying the nesting site of the stone curlew – well who needs them? Noisy, useless birds. I mean have you seen the mess they make of the microwave if you try to roast them?'

'Eurgh!' went up a cry – mainly from the girls – and a sly glint crept into Cassandra's eye.

'And if your dad is worrying about going out of business, Pravi Patel, he should cut his prices and so should yours, Bromley,' was her final piece of advice.

There was a lot of booing and hissing, but Cassandra seemed to relish it.

When it came to the vote, however, only three people raised their hands in favour of the Whoppa-Shoppa: Cassandra herself and her two friends whose free arms she had been twisting behind their backs in deadlocks.

'Yeah, but this lesson isn't the real thing, is it? You wait till the proper meeting tonight. Everyone will be backing WhoppaShoppa!' threatened the Washbone.

'What a loada rubbish!' chanted everyone, before Mr Gibbons managed to regain control of proceedings.

On the way out of school, Melvin caught up with Pravi.

'See you later, Pravi . . .? To help me get my bike back . . .?'

'Yeah. Right.'

'And you've got a rope?'

'My dad has.'

'Great.'

'Melvin . . .?'

'Yes?'

'It's not going to be dangerous, is it?'

When it came to danger, Pravi subscribed to Perkins' First Law of Survival (Keep Your Head Down). For him, as for Melvin, danger was all right so long as it was safely confined to the pages of *The Giant Vole of Gordian.*

'Not if we stay the right side of the wall. Don't worry, we can reach the bike from the top of the wall. I don't intend going inside there and coming face to face with that great brute again.'

'I hate dogs.'

'I wasn't thinking of the dog so much as its owner. He was a psycho. Fists of steel, multi-coloured tattoos and eyes that were sort of blank. No, I don't ever want to clap eyes on him again . . .'

They had just thrust open the double doors to take a short cut along the back of the hall, when Melvin stopped in mid sentence. The hall was being prepared for that evening's SSNOTS meeting. On the stage, behind a table and chairs and the stage curtain, there stood a giant wide-screen television monitor some two and a half metres square. The great brute of a man securing it in place had fists of steel, multi-coloured tattoos and eyes that were sort of blank. Melvin double-backed through the doors. Pravi followed.

'Melvin?'

'I just have!'

'Just have what?'

'Clapped eyes on him again! The guy rigging up that wide-screen telly. It's the Psycho!'

Pravi peered through the glass door. 'I see what you mean. He makes the Terminator look like a "Blue Peter" presenter!'

'What's he doing in school?'

'Perhaps he's the new PE supply teacher,' grinned Pravi.

'Pravi! I'm serious!' Melvin's desperate tone caught Pravi off guard.

'Okay, okay! He's setting things up for the meeting. The Washbone said it was going to be a recording studios!'

Pravi shrugged.

'Come on,' said Melvin, 'he gives me the creeps. Let's go the long way round.'

At the front door, Pravi headed for the changing rooms to get ready for cricket practice. Melvin made for the main gate. On his way past the teachers' car park he caught sight of a white van. A Dobermann pinscher sat upright on the passenger seat: alert, panting, eager.

No Zho'neng-Do. No house music. No games of Families. The Perkins' household was quiet. Just a series of indistinct mutterings from behind the closed sitting-room door: Melvin's mum and sisters were watching their favourite Australian soap. He sat down and opened *The Lay of the Dork: The Sixteenth Saga: The Giant Vole of Gordian.*

Murphin the Grule, sage of the Brummis, peered deep into his crystal goblet. 'Beware the tribe of Gordian Voles . . .'

The phone rang. And carried on ringing. It was obvious that no one in the sitting room was going to answer it.

'Hello?' said Melvin.,

'Melvin?' said Pravi's voice on the other end. 'Sorry.'

'What?'

'I can't make it – to help get your bike back. I've got to help my mum in the shop. My dad's going to the SSNOTS meeting. To put the case for the High Street shops against the WhoppaShoppa. Sorry.'

'Yeah. You've said.'

'Sorry.'

'Yeah.'

As Melvin put the phone down, the sitting-room

door was flung open to let out a warbling blast of the soap opera's theme tune.

'Oh sugar! Is that the time?'

'Mum, it's *always* this time when "Cobblers" – or whatever it's called finishes.'

'My notes! Where are my notes!'

'Under the hamster's cage.'

'Oh yes ... Right ... The developers are going to regret ever holding this public meeting tonight, Melvin. Roger Purkiss has estimated the extra amount of traffic through the town it will entail – and he's used a scientific model!'

'Wow!' said Melvin, but in her enthusiasm, his mum failed to notice his tone of sarcasm.

'The Nature people have provided us with all the details on the wart-biter ...'

'So called because legend has it that its bite can cure warts.'

Melvin's mum paused in mid-breath. 'You know?'

'Yes, Mr Gibbons told us at school.'

'Melvin, you should really come along to the meeting. Sounds like you know how to put Whoppa-Shoppa UK to shame!'

Perkins' First Law of Survival flashed its familiar warning through Melvin's head.

'Nah ... Nah!'

'Melvin, they may have big money, but we have the facts. Everyone in Smallham is behind SSNOTS,' his mum gushed excitedly.

47

'Except Cassandra Washbone,' muttered Melvin.

'We're going to beat them, Melvin!'

'I hope so, Mum,' said Melvin, his doubts show-ing. He thought of the tattooed thug putting up the TV monitor in the school hall – and the Dobermann pinscher. If this was the kind of person his mum and her SSNOTS committee were up against, he didn't rate her chances too highly.

'Oh, we're going to beat them, Melvin, make no mistake about that!'

VI

The Chief Executive of WhoppaShoppa UK sits on the platform at the top of the Sir Norman Burke Middle School hall. To his left sits the Chairperson of Smallham Town Council, who has been introduced to him as Councillor Mrs Wendy Washbone. On her left sits a rather nervous woman whose name he hadn't quite caught, but who was apparently Secretary of a protest group calling itself 'Smallham Says NO To Shopping-centre'. Behind him looms a gigantic wide-screen television monitor.

He studies the vase of scented roses on the table in front of him. He shudders. He has never been able to abide fresh flowers. Plastic ones, now that's another matter. Yes, deadheading's the only thing roses are fit for. He turns away from them and looks up beyond the vase towards the sea of summery faces filling the hall.

Yes, he thinks to himself, deadheading's the only thing they're fit for, too.

6

'Brushed against the finest thread of a spider's web . . .'

Melvin trudged up Hogman's Hill. He knew he couldn't retrieve his bike without Pravi and his rope – there wasn't even a way of getting in – but Hannah was not his idea of an ideal babysitter. Better to be out of the house, than in. He would do a recce; just suss a plan out for whenever he could next get Pravi up to HO HO HO to help him.

Bright yellow SSNOTS posters filled sitting-room and bedroom windows the whole length of his route.

He carried on walking until the wall surrounding the grounds of HO HO HO turned in at right angles along the edge of the Thorn. He snatched at the rye grass – and found it wasn't there. It had been trodden down by heavy feet. Feet that appeared to have clambered over the fence that took over where the wall left off: feet that appeared to have stomped through the Thorn right alongside the north wall of HO HO HO.

Melvin pondered upon Perkins' First Law of Survival (Keep Your Head Down) and decided there was no danger, providing he kept to the Thorn, which was public land after all. Dry twigs crackled under his feet. Here and there branches had been

50

snapped out of the way. Until about twelve metres in, he came to a massive oak tree. Here the tracks stopped. Melvin looked up. A sturdy branch hung low over the ground of HO HO HO. Tied to the end of the branch was a long rope.

There was no way Melvin was going to let himself into the grounds, not with Psycho and his Dobermann guarding the place. Anyway, a rope, no matter how long, was going to be of no use unless Pravi Patel was holding onto one end of it.

Or perhaps it was . . .?

Suddenly Melvin tumbled to the fact that the rope, tree and wall presented him with a better solution to getting his bike back without Pravi's help, thank you very much. He swung himself up onto the branch and inched his way along. The rope was only roughly tied and he undid the knot easily. Then folding the rope over his shoulder, the way he had seen mountaineers doing it on the telly, he backed up along the tree and slithered down onto the top of the wall.

Then he began to crawl along the top of the wall, first back to the road, then gaining confidence with every metre covered, along to the place where he had left his bike.

Oh, let his bike be there!

One or two cars sped by, their drivers peering out of their windscreens at him, but he was oblivious to them. All the time though, he strained his ears for the sound of a Dobermann.

Then he saw his bike.

Just as he had left it, leaning against the wall. Melvin closed his eyes with relief. 'Thank you,' he murmured. 'Thank you.'

'Please don't mention it, Perkins,' called a familiar voice below him.

'Arnold Thomas!'

'I gave my word that it would be here. And so it is.'

'It would've been more to the point if you'd given me a hand with it in the first place.'

'I did tell you that I couldn't.' Arnold sighed. 'I had rather hoped, Perkins old chap, that by now you might have fathomed the reason why.'

'What I've "fathomed" is this,' replied Melvin tetchily, still clinging to the top of the wall, 'there's no way your aunt would've sent you to live in this place on your own. You're a lying little toad, Arnold Thomas. Now move out of the way and let me swing the hook of this rope around my bike saddle.'

Arnold immediately sat himself on the saddle. 'Perkins, I trusted you to have thought better of me than to presume I would lie to you about my presence here.'

'I said get out of the way! I'll knock you off my bike else!'

'You won't,' said Arnold.

'I mean it!'

'I have no doubt that you do, for you are a spirited sort of fellow, but there is simply no way you can knock down a . . . a . . .'

'A what? A sneaky liar? A Fruit Cake?'

The two boys stood glowering at each other, daring each other, before Arnold spoke. Quietly.

'. . . A ghost.'

A ghost. Melvin looked fearfully into the other boy's pale impassive face and found he could not speak.

'For a ghost is what I am.'

Melvin sensed somehow that what Arnold had just told him was the truth. And the strange thing was, the more he looked at Arnold, the more his fearfulness receded. If you'd seen Melvin at that moment, you would have said he resembled not so much a person who had just seen a ghost, but someone who had just found a friend. Now that he knew Arnold was neither a compulsive liar nor a Fruit Cake, Melvin felt a profound sense of relief.

'So, knock me from your bicycle, Perkins,' Arnold was saying, 'and you will see I shall come to no more harm than I did from that wild dog – or his master.'

But Melvin didn't dare. Instead, slowly, he crouched on the wall, then reached down and put out his hand to touch Arnold. Instinctively Arnold put out his hand to shake Melvin's. Melvin's hand felt the faintest of sensations as the ghost took it in his; a warm tingling as if his palm had brushed against the finest thread of a spider's web.

'That is why I couldn't help you with your bicycle,' said Arnold. 'I have no physical power.'

'And is that why the guard didn't see you?'

Arnold nodded.

'Can anyone else see you?'

'Only the dog.'

'The dog?'

'Yes. It saw me just after you had escaped over the wall the other day.'

'So that was why it was whimpering.'

Arnold looked hard at Melvin. 'You are disturbed by what you see?'

'No . . . no!' said Melvin.

'Then climb down off that wall and join me.'

Melvin shook his head. 'I don't want to end up as a dog's dinner.'

'Neither the dog nor his surly master are here,' said Arnold.

No, thought Melvin suddenly, of course they're not! They're at the public meeting in the school hall. Melvin felt suddenly uneasy again about the WhoppaShoppa public meeting. He tried to put such thoughts from his mind. It was stupid, he knew; there was no way his mum was going to be attacked by a Dobermann – or its master – in a crowded school hall.

He slid down the wall onto his bike.

'Over the years,' said Arnold casually, 'I have found that it is mainly cats and dogs that have been aware of my presence.'

Melvin felt not a little crushed.

'How old are you?' he asked.

'Twelve, next Lady Day.'

Melvin frowned. 'I mean . . . what year were you born?'

'Eighteen sixty-nine.'

'And that story about your aunt sending you here . . . that's true?'

'Perfectly true. I'd got among a set whose pastime was dipping, d'you see?'

Melvin didn't. 'You mean they liked going for a swim?'

Arnold laughed. 'I mean they liked dipping their hands into other people's pockets.'

'You were a pickpocket?'

'You said that, I didn't. Anyways, at that time, this place was a school. Though, of course, it's been altered somewhat since then. Does your ma send you to school?'

Melvin nodded.

'I feel for you, Perkins. This school was known as Flogmore Hall and it was a name of which they were proud. If you answered back; if you were seen talking to the other boys; if you cried for your ma; if you piddled your bed – the punishment was always the same: a flogging. Can you believe it?'

Melvin could. He had heard plenty of people on the television saying that what young people needed to teach them respect was a good birching.

'So why come back here as a ghost if it was such a dreadful place?'

'Do you think that I *choose* to drift about this place, the scene of misery and torment for me? I haven't "come back" to this place. I have never left it. I died here.'

Melvin took a few steps back. Something unpleasant was going through his mind. He knew, from having 'done' the Victorians in history at school, that nineteenth-century children often died of hideous contagious diseases. He looked at Arnold's pale face ... could you catch a fatal disease from a ghost?

'Er ... what did you die of?'

'I didn't die *of* anything, Perkins.' Arnold paused. 'I was murdered.'

Melvin shivered, though he didn't notice. It was beginning to grow dark in the grounds of HO HO HO, but he didn't notice. He just sat by his bike, enraptured by his new-found ghost-friend's story.

'A new fellow was brought to Flogmore Hall. A mere shrimp of about six years of age. A little beggar. He told me of a reverend gentleman in Horsham who had made his concern the conditions faced by boys such as we in schools like Flogmore

Hall. We were caught talking, of course, and both flogged for our misdemeanour. I determined then to make my escape from Flogmore Hall and go to Horsham to alert this reverend gentleman of the scandal of ill-treatment and barbarism taking place here. Alas, I was caught. And it was that flogging, crueller than anything I had known before, which did for me.'

'And were your murderers caught?'

'The Master and his wife? Never. My death was put down as another case of pneumonia.'

'And didn't any of the other boys get to tell the truth about Flogmore Hall?'

Arnold shook his head. 'On leaving Flogmore for the wider world, they fell variously into two camps. Those who were intimidated and told that if they dared ever to say a word against the place they would be got at: they believed that and they were probably right. Then there were those who had learnt the only lesson Flogmore Hall had to offer and had become as hard and as brutal as the Master. For the suffering of others they cared nothing.'

'What about the "Shrimp" who told you about the vicar in Horsham in the first place?'

'Very much of the first camp. His beatings left him with a leg that would never work properly. He went off to sell matches on the promenade at Brighton, so I believe.'

'Do you think you will always be a ghost here?'

'Unless I can finally be at peace, indeed yes.'

'What do you mean, "at peace"?'

'Unless my murder is avenged.'

'How can it be? The people who did it must've died ages ago themselves.'

'It has to be. It just has to be.'

Melvin shifted himself and found that his legs were stiff from having been sitting for so long. He stood up and for the first time realised just how late it was getting.

'Hell's bells! I've got to be going!'

Melvin knotted the rope around his bike's handlebars. Then he climbed onto his bike and scrambled onto the top of the wall. Sitting astride the wall, he pulled his bike up and over the wall, grazing both arms in the process.

'You'll be back, won't you, Perkins?'

'With that dog patrolling the place?' Although in truth, there was nothing Melvin would have liked more than to find out more about Arnold and Flogmore Hall.

'I've told you. I can deal with the dog.'

'Yeah ... Well ...' Melvin wasn't convinced. 'I'll see. 'Bye.'

'You must come back!' There was a desperate urgency to Arnold's voice.

Melvin slid down the outside of the wall. He undid the rope. It ought to go back where it belonged, he supposed, but he hadn't time for all that. He threw it down into the grass and got onto his bike.

That was when he heard the voice on the other side of the gates: 'Oi! Perkins, you thieving moron! Come back here with my rope!'

Melvin turned and looked incredulously at the locked gates of HO HO HO. They were being rattled and shaken furiously.

'Look! I want to get out!'

'I should think you do, Washbone. There's a psychopath about to turn up with his Dobermann soon.'

'You've nicked my rope!'

'Borrowed it, Washbone. I was just going to put it back . . .'

'Frigging liar!'

Melvin thought of the ketchup incident. He thought of his vow to pay the Washbone back.

'See you, Washbone!' he called.

Then he pedalled off down the hill out of sight, Cassandra's shrill cursing echoing in his ears.

He got halfway down Hogman's Hill before he stopped his bike. He couldn't hear the Washbone's shrieks any more. He ought to pedal on he knew; leave her screaming for mercy at the feet of the Psycho and his dog. But . . . but . . . it was her rope after all and that dog was well dangerous . . . and . . .

The truth was, of course, that Melvin was

no P.W.S.T.

He turned his bike round and made his way back up the hill. When he got to the end of the wall, he got off and quietly made his way back along the grass verge to the gates of HO HO HO. Cassandra was slumped on the drive. He could hear her muffled sobs.

'I can't get you out over the gates, Washbone, 'cos of the spikes.'

Cassandra looked up.

'Go along to the corner of the wall. I'll chuck you the end of the rope.'

Without a word, Cassandra did as she was told. Melvin knotted the other end to the top bar of the gate. 'Up you come!'

The rope went taut with the strain. Melvin's knot began to slip at first; then held fast.

'Come on!'

First one hand appeared over the wall, then another, then Cassandra's head and shoulders.

'Now jump. No! Not like that . . .'

'Don't tell me how to jump, Perkins . . . aarghhh!' Cassandra landed with an ugly thud onto the grass verge and her shoulder bag bounced down heavily on top of her. 'I've ricked me flipping ankle! Don't just stand there like a lemon, help me up!'

Melvin wasn't quite sure how or where to try and lift Cassandra up. So he tried pulling her arm.

'Careful! I don't want me arm pulled out of its

socket as well! Lift me for goodness' sake, under me arms...'

Melvin put his hands under her armpits and lifted as Cassandra tried to push herself up with her good foot.

'What have you got in that bag? Rocks?'

'Mind your own business.'

After what seemed to Melvin like a lifetime, she was up.

'Who were you talking to in there, Melvin Perkins?'

Melvin's heart skipped a beat. 'Eh...? Er... no one.'

'Talking to yourself, were you?'

'Er... must've been.'

Cassandra shot Melvin a look full of doubt.

'I can't walk back down to Smallham like this,' she moaned. 'Can I sit on your bike?'

Leaving her propped against the wall on one leg, Melvin wheeled his bike to her. Resting on her good foot, she managed to swing into the saddle.

'I'll hold the saddle for you if you like, it'll be steadier that way,' suggested Melvin.

'Don't bother yourself, Lassie,' said Cassandra suddenly.

Without warning, she shoved Melvin in the chest, then stood up with both feet on the pedals and shot off down Hogman's Hill before you could say P.W.S.T.

'See you at school, Lassie!' she yelled over her shoulder.

'Washbone! Washbone! Come back here, you . . .!'

As he trudged back down the hill in the growing darkness, Melvin kicked himself for not having left Cassandra Washbone to the mercies of the Psycho and his dog.

By the time he crossed the High Street and turned up Dog Lane towards his house, his head hurt with all the questions spinning round it. Why could he and no one else, certainly not the Washbone, see and hear Arnold? Why was Arnold so desperate to see him again – could a ghost be lonely? How would he get his bike back (again)? How do you bring to justice a murderer who'd been dead for a hundred years?

In fact, so engrossed was Melvin with these mega-questions, he failed to notice that every sitting-room and bedroom window which had sported a bright yellow SSNOTS poster earlier that evening was now completely empty.

VII

'... *Mr Summerskill. Your company may have big money, but we have the facts – and we have the support. As secretary of SSNOTS, let me tell you, the people of Smallham will never, never allow this proposed development to take place!' Melvin's mum beats the air with her fist. Then she sits down.*

'Here! Here!' cries the audience, bursting into spontaneous applause. Slowly, one by one, they leap up to give Melvin's mum a standing ovation.

When the applause has died down, Councillor Mrs Wendy Washbone rises to her feet. 'This is going to be a formality, I'm sure, but we must let our hosts this evening put their case. I call on Mr Harry Summerskill, Chief Executive of WhoppaShoppa UK.'

Harry Summerskill stands up. 'Ladies and gentlemen,' he says. 'I have a video which I would very much like you to see.'

Without another word, he turns sharply round, slides a video into the VCR that sits beneath the giant wide-screen television monitor and presses the button marked PLAYBACK. Then he sits down, a malevolent smile curling about his thin lips.

7

'What about the *what*, dear . . .?'

'Is that you, Melvin?'

His mum was busy burning toast.

'Yes, Mum. Sorry I'm late. I had to walk back.' (Perkins' Third Law of Survival: Get Your Retaliation in First).

'Where's your bike then, dear?'

Relief: no ten-minute lecture on what he hadn't listened to his mum saying at breakfast or tea.

'Er . . . I left it with a friend.'

'Again? Who is it with this time?'

'Cassandra Washbone.'

Wait for the chortle, Perkins.

'Councillor Washbone's girl?'

'Yeah.'

No chortle.

'I didn't know you two were friendly.'

'We're not.'

'Then why . . .?'

'Don't ask, Mum. Just don't ask.'

'All right, Melvin, I won't ask.' She paused. 'To tell you the truth I was rather hoping you'd have asked *me* by now.'

'Asked you what?'

'Don't you want to know how *I* got on?'

It seemed to Melvin that there was very little point in asking his mum how she had got on. A swift glance in her direction showed a permanent smile radiating from her face. It was obvious she had scored a stunning success and the evil barons of WhoppaShoppa UK had been sent packing. Nevertheless, just to show form, Melvin asked, 'How did you get on, Mum? You weren't savaged by a Dobermann, were you?'

'Eh? No ... but the meeting went wonderfully well.'

'Great.'

'Harry ... Harry Summerskill, you know from WhoppaShoppa ...? What a very nice man. He showed us a lovely video. His development sounds so exciting ...'

'Mum?'

'All the shops in the new development will be open twenty-four hours a day!'

'Mum, you hate shopping!'

'And there'll be a burger bar ...'

'Mum! You're a fish-eating vegetarian.'

'... Together with parking for six hundred cars ...'

'Mum? What about the wart-biters?'

'What about the *what*, dear?'

'And the stone curlews. And the traffic ... you went on about it enough. The extra traffic through

65

the High Street . . .'

'We won't have to use the High Street, dear. Everything we need will be at the new Centre.'

'Then what will happen to Bromley the butcher's and Patel's?'

'Oh, Dennis Bromley and Ash Patel were both in favour of the WhoppaShoppa. In fact, when Harry Summerskill called for a show of hands, everyone was! There's going to be another meeting next Monday. WhoppaShoppa's what we need.'

'Mum? What has happened to you?'

'What do you mean, dear?'

'What about SSNOTS?'

'Now don't be rude, Melvin!'

'The "Say NO to the Shopping-centre" campaign.'

'What are you on about, Melvin?'

His heart in his mouth, Melvin raced through to the sitting room to rip the poster from the front window. He pulled back the curtain. Where there had earlier been a bright yellow poster, now there was nothing. He suddenly felt very sick.

'Melvin, are you quite all right?'

'Mum . . . the yellow . . .'

Melvin was looking straight into his mum's eyes.

They were as lifeless and as hard as a pair of buttons.

VIII

There are four of them sitting round the farmhouse table: three men and a woman. Their faces are all filled with the same crushing hardness. Angela speaks first.

'Did everything go according to plan?'

'Of course.'

'But they'll need topping up?'

'Yes. That isn't a problem, Darius. Another "public meeting" has been arranged. Then as soon as the "shopping-centre" is up, they'll be under our total control.'

'Good. Nothing can go wrong now then . . .'

'Nothing, Guy. Nothing. The deadheading process has begun.' The Chief Executive of WhoppaShoppa's lips curled into an ugly smile. 'There is nothing now that can be done to stop it.'

8

'The world ... turned upside down.'

'Melvin Perkins!'

Melvin stopped halfway up the corridor to 7GG's tutor room. Pravi marched up towards him. 'You've got my copy of *The Giant Vole of Gordian*,' he said, accusingly.

'Yeah ... I haven't quite finished it yet.' Somewhat taken aback by Pravi's tone, Melvin wasn't going to say that he hadn't even started it.

'How long does it take you to read a book, thickhead? I want it back, tomorrow.'

'Pravi ... ?'

Pravi marched on. Melvin frowned; deep in troubled thought. He'd never known Pravi to speak to him like that before. He sighed. Who else could he confide in about his multitude of worries: the fact that he'd made friends with a ghost, his mum had gone all funny-peculiar and Cassandra Washbone had possession of his bike?

He caught hold of the tutor room door just in time as Pravi let it swing back in his face. The place was buzzing.

'My mum says the WhoppaShoppa will be open twenty-four hours a day!' said Kayleigh Foster.

'My dad says there's going to be a video shop as big as Tesco's,' said Damien Higgins.

'My nan says it's like a palace – they showed a video,' said Jodie Jenkins.

'What about the wart-biters?' piped up Melvin, surprising even himself. The rest of 7GG stopped their chattering and looked up. They weren't used to Melvin Perkins voicing an opinion – and neither was he.

'My mum says they're going to catch them and move them to a site near Bognor Regis,' said Kayleigh.

'How would you like to be forcibly moved – and to Bognor Regis of all places?' asked Melvin. 'More to the point, how are they going to catch them? Have you ever tried catching a wart-biter?'

'I'm only telling you what my mum says.'

Melvin caught sight of two people sitting glumly at their desks at the back of the room: Pravi, who seemed to be engrossed in his maths homework and Sarah Jupe, who was staring glumly out of the window.

'And what about all the extra cars and lorries up and down the High Street? You heard what Sarah said when we had that debate in class yesterday!'

Sarah Jupe looked up. 'My mum's all in favour of the WhoppaShoppa now.'

'She can't be!'

'She left our house saying she was going to make

69

sure there would be no more lorries thundering down Smallham High Street. She said she was going to fight the WhoppaShoppa development all the way,' Sarah paused, then added quietly, 'for our Jamie's sake.'

7GG looked at their feet. They were not used to talking about death, particularly when it affected one of their own tutor group. Even though it was over eighteen months ago since Sarah's younger brother had been knocked down by a lorry on the High Street, they still approached her warily and with a certain degree of embarrassment.

'When she got back from last night's meeting at school, she told Dad and me that the Whoppa-Shoppa was a great idea. That a few more lorries in the High Street wouldn't make a scrap of difference and that anyway, we wouldn't have to use the High Street because everything we needed would be in the WhoppaShoppa. WhoppaShoppa's what we need, she said.'

'That's what my mum said,' said Kayleigh.

'And mine,' said Damien.

'Mine too,' muttered Melvin. 'In fact, those were her words exactly.' He sighed. 'And she is – was – the secretary of SSNOTS.'

The door crashed open, making everybody jump.

'See! What did I tell you lot yesterday? As soon as the WhoppaShoppa people put their case, everyone in Smallham would be in favour of them. And was I right or was I right, eh?' Cassandra Washbone marched down the class, punching the air triumphantly. 'I didn't see one SSNOTS poster up on the way to school!'

Melvin took his seat next to a silent Pravi.

'Oi, Perkins!' boomed Cassandra. 'Come round to my place after school, I've got something for you . . .!'

A communal 'Wer-hay!' shot up from the rest of the tutor group.

'Oo, Cassandra darling, I can't wait,' replied Melvin, without thinking – and shocking himself for the second time in as many minutes. Another 'Wer-hay!' went up. Melvin didn't have time to find out what the Washbone had to say to that, because Mr Gibbons strode in and called for a bit of a hush.

It was not until the bit of hush happened, that Melvin realised that he had just answered the Washbone back. What was happening? The world was turning upside down. Everybody – or at least their parents – seemed crazy for the WhoppaShoppa. Pravi had the sulks for the first time ever and now he, Melvin Perkins, had broken his own First Law of Survival (Keep Your Head Down) twice – and before the Gibbon had even had time to call the register!

Melvin swallowed hard as a now familiar feeling raced from the pit of his stomach to the back of his throat. He had felt it the night before when he had

71

seen his mum's eyes. He had thought that coming to school would've helped, but it hadn't, for he had felt it more strongly a few moments before, as his classmates had chatted excitedly about their parents' new-found enthusiasm for the Whoppa-Shoppa.

A feeling that was making his forehead sweat.

A feeling that could only be described as fear.

IX

In the sound-proofed studio behind the blacked-out windows of HO HO HO, banks of video screens flicker and flash nervously; tape decks babble and burble at speed.

'Everyone of them a deadhead,' Harry Summerskill grins, slyly. Then he shivers, suddenly, involuntarily. 'It feels cold in here tonight, Darius.'

'Yes, I thought that. Perhaps there's a door or window open.'

'There can't be. Everything's locked for security.'

The reason for the two men's discomfort slips away outside into the all-embracing blanket of the night. If he could have done so, he would have shivered too, not from cold though, but from a more terrifying sensation. Being without a living body, the ghost of Arnold Thomas can't feel sensations of warmth or cold, but he can sense atmospheres.

And he had sensed a particular kind of atmosphere more than strongly in the darkened studio.

The kind of atmosphere that can only be described as evil.

9

'WhoppaShoppa's what we need ...'

'Pravi!'

Pravi did not heed Melvin's call, but carried on slouching across the playground. Melvin caught up with him and grabbed him by the shoulder.

'Leave off, Perkins!'

'I see. Surnames is it now, Patel?' Melvin glowered hard at his friend.

Pravi blinked. 'What's got into you, Perkins? You've been yelling your head off all morning.'

'What's got into *you*, Patel?'

'My dad's going to go bust, all because your stupid mother couldn't get her SSNOTS act together and you ask me what's wrong!'

Melvin was stung by a sudden sense of protectiveness. 'Don't you call my mum stupid, stupid!' He shoved Pravi hard against the playground wall.

Pravi shoved him back.

Melvin took hold of his arm, roughly. Pravi grabbed Melvin's jacket and pulled him closer. Two pint-sized boys with bright haircuts and immaculate school uniform descended on Melvin and Pravi like a pair of vultures.

'Fight! Fight!' they squealed.

Chatter, chasing, games of football and space wars all stopped and everyone made for Melvin and Pravi.

'Fight! Fight!'

Melvin and Pravi were rolling on the ground desperately trying to punch each other. Melvin was conscious of the screaming, of the crowd drawing closer, then suddenly his head was jerked back, the sky flashed across his eyes and he was on his feet with a giant fist clutching his shirt collar. Pravi was on his feet too, and there was a giant fist clutching his shirt collar. The fists belonged to Miss Brownlow (PE and Netball).

Esther shook his head from side to side like a tennis umpire. 'Melvin Perkins, Pravikumar Patel, I am singularly disappointed in you both. What is the cause of this? Neither of you are boys known for fighting . . .'

Not known for fighting? I have never been in a fight before in my life, thought Melvin. Why hadn't he done like he usually did, muttered Perkins' First Law of Survival (Keep Your Head Down) to himself and walked away? What was happening to him?

'Which of you is responsible for initiating this fracas?' Esther was asking.

'I am, sir,' mumbled Pravi.

'No you're not, I am!' retorted Melvin. There I

75

go again, he thought.

Esther interrupted quickly, seemingly afraid that the two boys might come to blows again on his new Turkish rug. 'I won't punish you this time, as it is a first offence for you both,' he said. 'Instead I expect you to shake hands with each other and say "I'm sorry, Melvin," "I'm sorry, Pravikumar." '

Esther closed the door on them.

'Are you going to shake hands with me and say you're sorry?' Melvin asked Pravi.

'Get off!' said Pravi. 'That Esther's a nutcase. Are you going to shake hands with me?'

'No way!' said Melvin.

Melvin crossed the middle finger of his right hand over his index finger and held up his hand in front of Pravi's face. Pravi did the same.

'Fains!' said Melvin.

'Fains!' said Pravi.

They slapped palms and both yelled, 'Yee-ehh!' before making off down the corridor.

'Melv? Where are you going? I thought we were going to get your bike back?'

'We are.'

'But Hogman's Hill's up there!'

'Oh, didn't I tell you? My bike isn't at Hogman's Thorn House any more.'

'Where is it then?'

'The Washbone's.'

Pravi had stopped in his tracks. 'What! You never said! I'm not coming with you!'

Melvin shrugged. 'Suit yourself.'

'What's it doing with the Washbone?'

So Melvin told Pravi about his fateful meeting with Cassandra at Hogman's Thorn House. When they reached the Washbone's modern terraced cottage, Melvin opened the tiny, squeaky gate, but Pravi stayed rooted to the pavement.

The Washbone's bright red door was opened by a student with hair as flat as a doormat and a silver ring glinting in his left ear: Cassandra's brother, Bunny.

'I've come for my bike,' said Melvin.

'Eh?'

'Cassandra er ... *borrowed* it.'

Bunny shook his head. 'Not our Cas.'

'She did!'

Bunny still shook his head. 'Nah ... our Cas wouldn't borrow anything. Nick it, yes; take it without asking, yes, but *borrow* it? Nah ...'

Melvin grinned. He was beginning to warm to the Washbone's brother. 'She took it without asking.'

'Ah, now you're talking. Mountain bike, fluorescent turquoise with purple stripes?'

'That's the one.'

'It's in the garage. Help yourself. You can't speak to the good lady herself, I'm afraid, she's gone off.'

She went off a long time ago, thought Melvin. 'I

didn't want to particularly,' he said.

'Wise man.'

Melvin nodded. How could a P.S.W.T. like the Washbone have such an intelligent brother? Oh well, no doubt people who've met our Hannah reckon the same about me, he thought.

As he pulled the bike out of the garage, he caught sight of something.

'Did you see that, Pravi?'

'What?'

'Not what; who! Darting round the corner out of sight. I think we've been followed!'

Suddenly, Melvin felt himself being spun round. Pravi had hold of his shoulders and was staring into his eyes.

'Hey, what are you doing?' protested Melvin.

'Checking your eyes. To see if they've gone like my dad's. But they haven't.'

Melvin looked straight back at Pravi. 'How do you mean like your dad's?'

'When he came back from the WhoppaShoppa meeting last night, his eyes had gone all sort of glazed over. And I thought, what with you changing; getting all hard and picking a fight . . .'

'You called my mum stupid.'

'Now you know why I'm so . . . '

'So what?'

'Scared, Melvin. Yes, scared. Looking at my dad is like looking at a *doll*.'

78

'I know.'

'You can't, Melv . . . you can't know. Not unless you've seen them.'

'My mum's are the same,' said Melvin quietly.

Pravi looked concerned. 'You never said!'

'Well I have now.'

'I keep asking him why he's suddenly changed his mind about the WhoppaShoppa.'

'And what does he say?'

'WhoppaShoppa's what we need. WhoppaShoppa's what we need.'

'That's exactly what my mum said last night. Exactly.'

'What's happening in this town, Melvin?'

'I don't know, Pravi, but I'll tell you something – the Washbone's involved in it, whatever it is.'

'How do you know?'

'Remember the debate at school yesterday? She *knew* that everyone would change their minds about the WhoppaShoppa development. And she's been hanging about Hogman's Thorn House. She told Kayleigh and Jodie it was a film studio making pop promos, but *we* know the truth: the people who've done the place up are the WhoppaShoppa people.'

'And why have you been going up there?'

'You don't think I've got something to do with it, do you?'

'You have changed.'

Melvin didn't – couldn't – deny his friend's

accusation.

'So why *have* you been going up there?'

Melvin took a deep breath. 'There's this kid lives up there . . .'

'In the old house?'

'Yeah, his name's Arnold Thomas.'

'What's he like?'

'All right. Talks a bit weird sometimes.'

'Do you mean a Cockney or something?'

'No, I mean he's a ghost.'

'A what?'

'A ghost.'

'Melvin . . .?'

'He was murdered.'

Melvin pushed the button and he and Pravi waited for the green man to appear so that they could cross the High Street.

'Melvin!'

'By his headmaster.'

'Melvin . . . !'

'Hello, Pravikumar! Hello, Melvin!' Sarah Jupe's mum was standing just behind them. 'Off to the library, are you?'

Melvin shook his head. The green man flashed excitedly hurrying them across.

'You should. They've got a wonderful exhibition on.'

Melvin sighed. Smallham Library was always having exhibitions, usually about the wonders of learning Icelandic basket weaving at evening class or the joys to be discovered in joining Smallham & District Country Dancing Circle.

'It's entirely devoted to the new WhoppaShoppa development!' Mrs Jupe gushed. She gave Melvin and Pravi a wave. 'WhoppaShoppa's what we need!'

Melvin gave her a horrified look and for the first time saw her eyes: they were looking in his direction, but not at him. And they were as hard and as unseeing as a pair of marbles.

'It's happening to everyone,' said Pravi.

Melvin shook his head. 'It's happening to everyone who was at the meeting last night.' He turned sharply up a narrow twitten that led to the Town Hall car park.

'Where are you off to now?'

'Where do you think? The library.'

Smallham Library was a square, red-brick Victorian building that had been occupied many years ago by the Primary School. Inside it was light and spacious with tall, thin windows. Huge grainy bookcases lined the walls, so tall and solid-looking that it seemed as if they actually held the library building up. It was once a place around which you walked on tip-toe, within which you spoke in whispers, but nowadays it buzzed with activity. Librarians clattered about on step-ladders filling up the shelves with books, computers bleeped, photocopiers whirred and while the people of Smallham chose their books, they chatted to each other; usually about the dreadful behaviour of young people today and how it was all the fault of their parents, teachers, television, computers, drugs and cheeseburgers.

Melvin and Pravi found the WhoppaShoppa exhibition covering a large area near the issues desk. Around the walls there were plans and glossy, colourful pictures depicting happy, smiling people in various parts of the WhoppaShoppa centre. There was also a large poster reminding people about next Monday's meeting.

On a table there was a model of the main WhoppaShoppa arcade. Pravi studied it closely. 'Keen on security, aren't they?' he said. 'Look there's two or three video screens in all the shops. And in the arcade . . .'

They were interrupted by the librarian.

'It's wonderful, isn't it?' she said. She looked at them with dull lifeless eyes, eyes that somehow didn't seem to belong to her. 'WhoppaShoppa's what we need.'

Melvin gave Pravi a desperate look. 'WhoppaShoppa's what we need. WhoppaShoppa's what we need,' he mimicked. 'It's like some sort of chant they've learnt . . .' He stopped suddenly. 'There's something odd about all this,' he muttered.

'What?'

'Well if I knew, I'd say, wouldn't I!'

'Would you?'

'Yes! Wait...!' Melvin knitted his brows and stared at the glossy artists' impressions of the WhoppaShoppa arcade. 'What do people do when they're walking down a shopping arcade?'

'Look for the nearest exit?' asked Pravi, unhelpfully.

'They look in the shop windows!'

'Oh yes...! But all the people in these pictures, their eyes are looking up, as if they were looking at the shop signs...'

'No!' said Melvin suddenly and loudly. He was studying the table-top model. 'No, Pravi, not the shop signs. Look! You'd got it sussed in the first place. Remember? Just before the librarian poked her nose in with her chant – "big on security, aren't they?" you said, or something like that. And you pointed to all the video screens: two or three in every shop and in the arcade...'

'So...?'

'If you've got a video security system, it's not video screens you need – except perhaps one by the till – it's *cameras*. And why have screens in the arcade?'

'For people to look at,' reasoned Pravi, 'while they're shopping. Like the Post Office.'

'Unless...' mused Melvin. 'I've just remembered something else my mum said when she came back from the meeting last night. *He showed us a lovely video.* Somehow the WhoppaShoppa lot have changed people's minds . . .'

'And eyes . . .'

'Using video. The Washbone's right. There is a film editing studio inside the house, but it's not for editing rock videos. It's for editing people's minds. To make them enthusiastic about the Whoppa-Shoppa.'

Pravi shook his head. 'How? Videos can't brain-wash you . . .'

'What about video nasties? My nan says watching them can turn you into a serial killer.'

'Only people who are psychos in the first place. Everyone at that meeting has been turned into a WhoppaShoppa lover! Even my dad. And he stands to lose his shop and everything. Anyway, it doesn't make sense.'

'What doesn't?'

'If the WhoppaShoppa people are somehow using video to make people like your mum and my dad support their new shopping-centre, why should they need video screens in the shopping-centre? I mean they'll have got what they want by then, won't they?'

'Unless, there's something else?'

'What?'

'I don't know. Something else they're going to do with all those video screens once the centre goes up.' Melvin was scared by the way his thinking was going. 'Perhaps they want to keep on editing people's minds, for the rest of their lives. If they could get your dad to change his mind about the WhoppaShoppa development, they could get him to do anything they wanted!'

Pravi shivered. 'I think we should go up to Hogman's Thorn House and see what else we can find out about the WhoppaShoppa organisation. That's where the studio is, isn't it?'

'Yeah . . .' Melvin's voice was full of doubt.

'Tonight?'

'Er . . . I'm doing something tonight.' Melvin knew there was only one person who might know about the workings of the film studio. But he couldn't afford to have Pravi around while he talked to the ghost of a murdered Victorian pickpocket.

'Cancel it! Crikey Mikey, Melvin, this is important! Something really scary and . . . *bad* is happening to my dad and your mum – and everyone else in Smallham, and you're too busy to find out what?'

Melvin pushed his chair away from the table and got up.

'Perkins' First Law of Survival, that's what it is, isn't it?'

'No!'

'You're scared!'

'You didn't have to scarper from that dog!'

'You were keen enough to drag me up there to rescue your precious bike. Is your bike more important than your mum – or my dad?'

'Okay, sorry. Tomorrow evening.'

Outside, Pravi turned to go back home to the High Street.

'Tell me this, Melvin Perkins. All that stuff about that ghost. It was a wind-up, wasn't it?' There was a bitter edge to his voice. He was trying to look into his eyes again, Melvin noticed.

'Yeah,' said Melvin, unlocking his bike.

'At least that's one thing about you that hasn't changed,' said Pravi darkly, turning sharply on his heels and stomping off towards the High Street.

'What?'

'You're still lousy at wind-ups.'

They were far too busy eye-balling each other to notice the brightly-clad figure dive round the side of the library.

X

The Chief Executive of WhoppaShoppa UK locks the door of Hogman's Thorn House and walks towards the black BMW.

'Good night, Gary.'

'Good night, Mr Summerskill.'

The security guard pulls at the leash around the dog's neck to quieten its snarls. Suddenly its ears prick up. Straining at the leash, it bares its sharp, yellowing teeth and begins to growl.

'Let it go, man! It's heard something!' shouts the Chief Executive of WhoppaShoppa UK.

The dog bounds off down the drive, growling menacingly. Then it stops. As it sees the pale outline of Arnold Thomas, its back legs skid underneath its belly and it lies on the tarmac, whimpering and cowed.

'What's wrong with the stupid animal?' screams the Chief Executive of WhoppaShoppa UK, as the guard dog slinks back to its master, tail between its legs.

'I dunno, Mr Summerskill.'

'Cut down on its food.'

'Yes, Mr Summerskill.'

'*Completely!*'

'*Yes, Mr Summerskill.*'

'*You're pampering that animal. It's losing its killer instinct. Let it fend for itself! A good guard dog is a hungry dog.*'

The Chief Executive of WhoppaShoppa UK slams the car door angrily behind him and with a squeal of tyres spins round and heads off down the drive.

10

'Light and dark, Perkins. Good and evil...'

The eyes stared back at him as big as pizza plates. They didn't scare him; they were his own. No, they weren't lifeless, dull or as hard as marbles, Melvin was sure of that. He turned away from his bedroom mirror and sighed. There was no doubt that Pravi was right though, he *had* changed, he knew. And that was the crucial difference: his mum, Pravi's dad and the others didn't know they'd changed. He felt the fear creeping up his gullet again.

He collided with Hannah on his way to the kitchen.

'Watch where you're going, stupid!'

'You're welcome!' replied Melvin with mock cheerfulness.

But Hannah was out of the front door without hearing him. She slammed it behind her and the ceiling lights swayed like lanterns on a storm-tossed boat. At least Hannah's behaviour hadn't changed.

'I'm going for a ride on my bike,' Melvin told his mum.

'That's nice, dear.'

Melvin waited for the inevitable earful: where are you going... don't be late... mind the traffic...

look after that bike, it was expensive . . . but his mum didn't reply. She simply smiled at him with her unseeing eyes, before drifting out of the kitchen and up the stairs.

Ellie took a break from her packet of crisps. 'She's in love,' she said, with a sigh.

'Who, Mum?'

'No, Hannah.'

'Oh.'

'With a boy.'

'That figures.'

'Called Warren.'

'How do you know this, Ellie?'

'I've heard her on the phone to him.'

The rope had gone from the grass verge. Melvin wasn't surprised. He guessed the Washbone had been back. He made his way to the big oak tree, as he had done the previous evening. No rope hung from the overhanging branch. Of course, it didn't, thought Melvin: the Washbone was keen to make sure nobody followed her. He clambered up on the branch and worked his way along. Then he heard a familiar voice below him.

'It's above your head.'

'Arnold?'

'I saw her put it there.'

Melvin looked up. Well hidden among the leafy branches and curled up neatly like a sleeping snake was the rope. Melvin secured it to the branch and dropped into the garden of HO HO HO.

'You were right to hide from her, Perkins.' Arnold's mood was sombre. 'She is a dangerous person.'

'I know that.'

'She comes here armed.'

'Armed?'

'With a gun.'

'A gun? The Washbone? Are you sure?'

'Don't take fright so, Perkins, she was here earlier, but she's not here now. I saw her holding a large gun. She was lining up the sights and pointing the barrel at the house. She was talking to herself. *I can get a good shot from here.* Those were her words, Perkins.'

Melvin gulped. Guns were things you saw on telly programmes, not in the hands of a classmate, even if she was the P.W.S.T.

'Did she shoot anyone?'

Arnold shook his head.

'Where's the dog?'

'Inside the house.'

Melvin shivered. 'Inside the house' was still uncomfortably close. 'Do you know what they're doing in there?'

'The old servants' quarters at the back have been filled with machines displaying moving pictures . . .'

'It's an editing studio,' said Melvin. 'That much

we know. What are the pictures of?'

'People.'

'Doing what?'

'Smiling, laughing – and it appeared, shopping. The man Harry speaks on the moving pictures . . .'

'What does he say?'

'Some kind of poetry.'

'Poetry?'

'Di dum di dum di dum WhoppaShoppa's what we need . . .'

'Is that all you can remember?'

'There are words on some of the pictures.'

'What do they say?'

'I don't rightly know.'

'Didn't you get a chance to read them or what?'

'Perkins,' said Arnold quietly, 'I can't read.'

'Didn't they teach you at Flogmore Hall . . .?'

Arnold gave a hollow laugh and shook his head. 'I may not be able to read letters, Perkins, but I can read an atmosphere. This house . . . Flogmore Hall . . . Hogman's Thorn House . . . the name is immaterial. This house and this land have power.'

'How do you mean?'

'Have you never felt the atmosphere of a building or a place?'

'Yes . . .' Melvin vividly recalled visiting Arundel Cathedral with his mum and Hannah, just after Ellie was born. 'Isn't it glorious!' she had said. But Melvin had looked up at the great solid shafts of sunlight bursting through the sky high windows to catch the millions of dust particles as they danced about the cavernous space and he had felt nothing but foreboding and unease. That had been a couple of weeks before he had last seen his dad.

'Yes . . .' said Melvin. 'Yes.'

'The South Downs are ancient, Perkins. Here the Romans built a temple to their gods. Here the old druids sang to the sun on Midsummer's morning.'

Melvin frowned.

'So perhaps we shouldn't be so surprised. That this house, this place, for whatever reason – can *empower* certain people.'

'Isn't that a good thing?' asked Melvin.

'Yes,' said Arnold. 'And no. Take a look through the trees at the building. Notice how it lies: facing towards the east.'

'So . . .?'

'On a summer's day; even a bright winter's day, the front of the house will be bathed in sunlight. But the back of the house has never received light at all. The slope of the wood rising up behind it and the speed with which the sun sets over the Downs prevents that. Light and dark, Perkins. Good and evil. Some are empowered for good; others for evil. The druids may have worshipped the sun up here, but witches also danced widdershins.'

'Widdershins?'

'Anti-clockwise, in a circle. To summon the devil.'

Melvin swallowed hard. 'Were you empowered when you tried to escape from Flogmore Hall?'

Arnold nodded. 'I found an inner strength of purpose I never knew that I had. Alas, that went for the Master too. His empowerment gave him the strength and the will to murder me.'

'So evil triumphed over good?'

'On that sad occasion, it did. Thus am I destined to haunt these grounds. Until such time as my murder is avenged.'

Melvin hung his head in the dark silence.

'Perkins. The people working magic with their moving pictures machinery have been empowered, too. And the inner strength and knowledge with which they have been empowered they are intent on using for evil. You must believe that.'

'I do,' said Melvin. 'Oh I do.' He told Arnold of the terrifying effect that attending the Whoppa-Shoppa public meeting had had on his mum and, it seemed, all the other people who had been there.

'They spoke about the people present at that meeting, Perkins. The man they call Harry and his accomplice. They laughed, a cruel laugh. They called them "deadheads".'

'Deadheads? That's what you cut off the top of roses,' said Melvin, but the more he thought about it, the more the words seemed to be an apt description of his mum's condition,

'That's what my mum is, Arnold. A deadhead.'

'I fear the very worst,' said Arnold. 'This man Harry has been empowered with the will, the inner strength and the knowledge to commit great evil.'

'And what about the Washbone with her gun? Has she been empowered by evil?'

'It would appear so.'

'I've been changed too, Arnold. I picked a fight with my mate Pravi, this morning, because he called my mum stupid.'

Neither of them spoke for a moment, then Arnold said quietly, 'And there is some power driving you. I can tell that.'

'That isn't power, Arnold. It's fear. Fear of what has happened to my mum. And to Pravi's dad. And fear of what else is going to happen to them.' He stared glumly at the ground. 'What else do you know about what goes on in the editing studio?'

'Only what I've told you.'

Melvin sighed.

'Isn't that enough?'

'To have any chance of stopping them, I need to know precisely what they are doing in there . . .'

'What do I understand of the mysteries of moving pictures? I, who cannot even read letters. No, you are better placed to fathom that, Perkins, being a child of your time.'

'Yes. But I'd have to get in first.' Somehow, Melvin didn't feel as if it was him speaking. Why didn't he just obey Perkins' First Law of Survival and go? He knew very well. His mum. Pravi's dad. So this is what empowerment means, he thought. What a nightmare.

Arnold was speaking. '. . . It would not be difficult to gain access.'

'Oh?'

'You see the iron fire escape at the back?'

'Yes . . .'

'A recent addition, of course. It leads to a skylight. Now the skylight itself has been made secure. But it is possible to lift the surrounding roof tiles and gain entry to the attic. A large ventilation grille in the attic floor will, providing you are in possession of a strong light, afford you a good view of the moving picture machinery immediately below.'

'Sounds like a job for two people.'

'Your friend – Pravi . . .?'

'Yes.'

'Good. They finish working their moving picture machinery by dusk at the latest.'

Melvin swallowed hard. 'What about the dog?'

'You need fear no harm from that creature while I am around. And at night, he's left inside. He'll not reach you in the attic.'

'Tomorrow night then.'

'Till tomorrow, Perkins.'

XI

The frantic cry of terror gives way to squealing pain. Then an uneasy silence quickly follows, broken only by the occasional throaty growl as the dog shakes the rabbit by its neck until it is dangling from its jaws like a piece of limp lettuce.

After tossing the dead animal about like a plaything, the dog drops it on the doorstep of Hogman's Thorn House and begins to rip the flesh from its bones with that voracious appetite peculiar to starved hunting beasts.

Which is why when a large, black BMW draws up a little later, the Chief Executive of WhoppaShoppa UK finds himself having to step over the stinking entrails of a dead rabbit in order to reach the front door.

'Sorry, Mr Summerskill,' mumbles the guard. 'I'll get the dog some proper food. I've got a couple of tins of Pal somewhere.'

'Nonsense,' snarls his boss. 'Like I've said before, a good guard dog is a hungry dog. Let it roam the grounds tonight.'

11

'Arnold, where are you? You can't let us down! Not now!'

'What have you got in that bag, Pravi?'

Melvin stopped his bike halfway up Hogman's Hill and watched his friend huffing and puffing to catch him up, a bulging bright red and blue rucksack hanging from his shoulders.

'I got . . .' Pravi stopped his bike too and struggled for breath. 'I got . . . me dad's tow rope and torch which *you* said we needed.'

'We do.'

'. . . And I've got my totems for survival.'

'Your what?'

'When the Chief Boagha of the Brummis goes forth in *The Lay of Dork*, he always takes his totems for survival.'

'His trusty stave and his grandma's magic tooth you mean?'

'Yeah . . . but I couldn't get a trusty stave to fit on my bike, could I?'

'And your gran hasn't got a magic tooth?'

'My gran hasn't got *any* teeth.'

Melvin recalled the times he'd been surprised by old Mrs Patel's gummy grin when he had been invited into Pravi's sitting room.

'Which reminds me,' said Pravi pointedly, 'you've still got my copy of *The Giant Vole of Gordian*.'

When they reached the Thorn, they hid their bikes in the undergrowth. The dying light cast strange shadows as it flickered through the trees.

'What did you tell your mum, Melvin?'

'Said I was at your place. She just said, "That's nice." What did you tell your folks?'

'Said I was at your place. My dad just smiled.'

'What's wrong, Pravi?'

'I wish I was, that's all.'

'You wish you were what?'

'At your place.'

'We've got to do it, Pravi. Finding out what's going on here is the only chance we've got of saving your dad and my mum and the rest of them from . . . from . . . whatever's . . .'

'Whatever's . . .?'

'Whatever's taken them over.'

Pravi shivered. 'Providing we don't get caught and find the same thing taking us over.'

'We won't get caught!'

Melvin didn't say anything about the dog. He still felt that his friend was putting a distance between them. There was no trust there any more.

When they reached the oak tree, Melvin climbed up first.

'Pass us the rope.'

He inched his way along the branch – and saw

something that made his mouth turn dry. Pravi was close behind and saw too.

'There's already one here!'

'Must be the Washbone's.'

'You mean I've lugged my dad's tow rope all the way up here for nothing?'

'No. We might need it. If she goes before we do, she'll take her rope with her.'

Melvin didn't say anything about his doubts as to whether the tow rope would be long enough to throw over the branch.

'She'll give us a right earful if she sees us.'

She'll give us more than that, thought Melvin, but he didn't say anything about her being armed. Images of the Washbone – a newly-empowered Washbone, wielding a gun; of the security man's callous leer; of the snarling Dobermann – flashed through his mind. Just for one moment, he thought of turning back. Then he thought of his mum; Pravi's dad – and the people who had deadheaded them.

'Come on,' he called to Pravi.

They swung down off the branch into the springy undergrowth. There was no sight nor sound of the Washbone. There was no sight nor sound of the dog. There was no sight nor sound of Arnold either. Keeping close to the inside of the garden wall, Melvin made his way towards the house. Pravi followed.

'Supposing there's someone inside the house?' asked Pravi, not for the first time, a note of real anxiety creeping into his voice.

'There's not!' The doubt in Melvin's voice was apparent. 'If there is, I'll know.'

'How?' Pravi was edgy.

Melvin turned towards his friend. 'I just will! All right?' His voice was edgy now. 'Now come on!'

Melvin turned back to face the house. And saw Arnold standing in his path.

'You must go back!'

'What?'

'I didn't say anything,' grumbled Pravi. It was obvious he could neither hear nor see Arnold.

'They're working late. They haven't left yet. And when they do, they'll let the dog out,' said Arnold.

'You said they kept it in at night!'

'Stop wittering to yourself,' said Pravi. 'You're giving me the creeps!'

'Shut up, Pravi, let me handle this!' snapped Melvin.

'You're mad, Melvin Perkins!'

'They've changed their practice,' said Arnold. 'And I can't protect you from the dog *and* the girl. She's over by the front door with her gun now!'

Hardly were the words out of Arnold's mouth, than a terrifying howl pierced the air. Crazed, insistent, frenetic; as only the howl of a hungry dog who has tasted blood can be.

'The dog!' muttered Melvin under his breath. 'Run!' he yelled, but when he turned he saw Pravi already crashing through the bushes back to the rope, his rucksack jiggling crazily up and down on his back.

Then came the scream.

'Cassandra!' mouthed Melvin silently.

'Run!' yelled Arnold to Melvin.

'Cassandra . . .'

'Why doesn't she shoot the damned animal!'

'Get the dog!' shrieked Melvin.

'Now, for the love of mercy, go!'

Another scream; then another howl filled the air.

'Go, Perkins!'

'Arnold! Stop the dog!'

The urgency of Melvin's plea sent Arnold flying off towards the house. Melvin charged bull-like, back through the bushes. He stumbled, felt his skin tear as it was snicked by gorse and wild rose bushes. *I'm in a nightmare that's what it is, that nightmare where you can't move your legs fast enough to get to where you're going.* Out of the corner of his tear-stained eye he caught sight of Pravi's rucksack hurtling over the wall and Pravi clawing at the rope.

He grabbed the rope in his sweaty palms. Despite the pounding in his ears, he could hear the Washbone's screams; each one more terrified, more insistent and louder than the last. That was when, with a feeling of utter sickness, he realised it wasn't just another nightmare: nightmares, however terrible, are silent. As he pulled hard on the rope, he heard another howl. *'Arnold, where are you? You can't let us down! Not now!'*

He reached the branch, glanced down and found himself staring into a pair of terrified, yet familiar eyes. She was on the far side of the rope. She had come through the bushes from the drive. *No wonder Arnold didn't find her; he went towards the house!* Then Melvin saw Cassandra raising her right arm.

'No, Cassandra! Don't shoot! Don't . . .'

Melvin caught his breath. In her hand she held not a gun, but a small, hand-held camcorder.

Arnold Thomas, you Victorian nano-brain!

Cassandra held the camcorder up for Melvin to take. She was shaking, breathless.

Melvin leant right over and grabbed the camcorder. Cassandra was already up the rope and had hold of the branch, but her breathlessness made her slow for the final pull up. There was a crash of breaking twigs and branches behind them, and out of the shrubbery leapt the panting Dobermann pinscher. It bared its teeth for a split second, before springing wildly at the girl's dangling ankles, all four of its legs off the ground.

'No . . . no!' Cassandra let out a terrified scream of pain as the dog's slavering jaw sank tight into her leg. As she flinched her hands began to slip slowly away off the branch. A hand appeared over

Melvin's shoulder and took the camcorder from him. '*Good man, Pravi.*'

Melvin grabbed hold of Cassandra's right hand. 'Just . . . hold . . .!' he yelled, not knowing how he could bear the girl's weight for a moment longer.

His words echoed eerily. For it was now quiet. The dog lay cowering underneath Cassandra's dangling legs, whimpering softly. Arnold stood between it and the girl.

Another arm appeared next to Melvin's: Pravi's. He took Cassandra's other hand.

'Come on, Cassandra, it's all right now,' coaxed Melvin. They managed to pull her up so that she could fold herself over the branch on her stomach. Sobbing all the time, she inched her way back along the branch behind Pravi. Pausing only to hitch up the rope, Melvin followed.

They had just reached the point where the branch passed over the wall, when Melvin heard a voice saying:

'Don't I get a word of thanks, Perkins?'

'Thanks, Arnold,' muttered Melvin.

'It's not over yet,' Melvin thought he heard Arnold say, just before he heard voices, getting closer, more animated.

'There was definitely someone screaming blue murder.'

'Probably that scrawny kid again, Mr Summerskill.'

104

Melvin recognised the guard's flat monotone.

'What scrawny kid?'

Melvin dropped down out of the tree the other side. Between them, he and Pravi shouldered Cassandra down.

'You tell me everything in the future! Everything! I'm not having my life's work fouled up by snooping kids, scrawny or otherwise!'

'No, Mr Summerskill – ' There was a pause. 'Mr Summerskill! Look!'

A pathetic whimpering filled the silence.

'What *is* wrong with the stupid animal? It's supposed to be a guard dog, not a poodle! Go on, get up, you lazy beast!'

There was a yelp. Melvin winced. Then came the sound of a snarl. Melvin supposed, quite rightly, that this was the moment Arnold had chosen to make his excuses and leave. Another snarl. Another yelp. This time human.

'Get that leash round it, man! Quick, it's got my hand!'

Sounds of scuffling. Then the thick, short, gasping growl of an angry dog with a leash tightening on its neck.

'Shall I search the bushes, Mr Summerskill?'

'For crying out loud, man, are you thick as well as stupid? Get me to a doctor quickly!'

The sounds faded into silence.

'Let's get down to the road,' whispered Melvin.

Cassandra was biting her lip in pain. She pointed to the top of the wall.

'The camcorder!' Pravi shinned back up the tree and grabbed it down. They heard a car purr down the drive and swing out onto the road. The sound of its engine died away as it made its way down Hogman's Hill toward Smallham.

Melvin and Pravi lifted Cassandra onto her good leg and helped her down through the trees to the road.

'I can't walk!' mumbled Cassandra, wincing with pain.

'That's what you told me the other evening,' said Melvin bitterly. 'Why not take my bike?'

'Melv!' said Pravi, shocked by his friend's callousness.

Then Melvin caught sight of Cassandra's leg. On her left calf, a mass of congealed blood showed where her jeans had been ripped away.

'Yeah ... well ...' Melvin sighed. He looked at Cassandra's leg again. 'Does it hurt?'

'Of course it bloomin' well hurts, stupid!'

'Sorry. Do you want a hankie?'

'Ta.' Cassandra took the hankie Melvin offered her and promptly blew her nose into it. 'Ta.'

''Salright,' shrugged Melvin. 'You can keep it.'

'What do we do now?'

'Hold on!' Pravi was ferreting around in his rucksack. 'I may not have a trusty stave or one of my grandma's magic teeth, but I do have . . .' Out came a mobile phone. 'This is my mum's. She takes it if she goes out in the car alone.'

He tapped out the digits. The phone burbled reassuringly. 'Hello? Mum? Pravikumar . . .!' Those were Pravi's last words of English for the next couple of minutes. Cassandra and Melvin glanced at each other: Pravi seemed to be getting an earful from his mum. Eventually, 'See ya then!' he said, and flicked the phone off.

'Mum's on her way. In the van. That way she can take the bikes.'

'Good man, Pravi.'

'Yeah,' mumbled Cassandra.

'What else did she say?'

'She said once she's dropped you two off, she's going to kill me.'

'Thanks, Pravi.'

'What a mess.'

'How did we manage to get out of there?' asked Cassandra. 'I mean how did I get up the rope and you two pull me up . . . how did we manage it?'

'We were empowered,' Melvin said, quietly.

'Eh?'

'Don't mind him,' replied Pravi, 'he's completely mad. He talks to ghosts, you know.'

'Pravi!'

But Cassandra wasn't laughing.

XII

There are four of them sitting round the gnarled farmhouse table: three men and a woman. Their faces are all filled with the same crushing hardness.

'Don't get so excited, Guy! Gary reckons there's been some kids snooping around that's all.'

'Kids are trouble. I should know. I spend all day teaching the little . . .'

'The tape's finished. We've cleared the studio of all evidence. Come the next meeting on Monday, stage one will be completed – and the deadheading programme will be irreversible. Now, Guy, relax!'

Guy grimaces. 'Monday evening I'll relax.'

12

'Melvin? It seems to be all down to you.'

Cassandra wasn't at school next day.

Melvin was too depressed, too shaken, to say very much to Pravi. They'd blown the chance of finding out what was really going on in HO HO HO and with it, any hope of halting whatever dreadful plans WhoppaShoppa UK had in store for the residents of Smallham.

His mum would be a deadhead for ever.

'Your mum still the same?' asked Pravi.

'Yeah.'

'My dad too.'

'Did you get told off?'

'When I told my mum I was only trying to save our shop, she burst into tears.'

'I hate it when grown-ups cry.'

When Melvin got home, Ellie said, 'Your girlfriend rang up.'

'I haven't got a girlfriend.'

'I've got a boyfriend,' said Ellie. 'We're going to get married and have lots of babies, so we can have a Range Rover. That'll be nice, won't it?'

'So long as you don't ask me to babysit,' replied

Melvin, wearily.

Melvin's mum came through. Melvin couldn't look her in the eyes any more, for fear he would start blubbing.

'Cassandra rang for you, dear. You're to go round to her house straight away. It sounded important.'

She opened the bright red door.

'Come on in,' she said.

'How's your leg?'

'They put a couple of stitches in. Lucky I had that tetanus jab last term.'

Melvin remembered the brawl during Maths, when Cassandra had got stabbed by a pair of compasses.

'Should be worth at least another week off school. Not bad, eh? We're in Bunny's room. The others are here.'

'Others?'

'Yes. Bunny, Sarah, Pravi . . .'

'Eh?'

'And – ' Cassandra winked slyly at Melvin as they reached the landing, 'you-know-who's here as well!'

'Who's you-know-who?'

'I think she's dead pretty,' whispered Cassandra, 'but don't tell her I said.'

'Who?'

Cassandra flung open the bedroom door.

'HANNAH!'

Hannah was sprawled out on a large beanbag, hugging Bunny Washbone's arm. Ellie's words leapt through Melvin's mind: *'She's in love . . . with a boy . . . called Warren.'* Bunny: Warren. Melvin groaned to himself.

'Make yourself at home, Melvin,' said Bunny.

Melvin sat down on the bed next to Pravi. Sarah and Cassandra sat on the floor. The walls of Bunny's room were covered with photographs, most of them black-and-white. Some were of cars and bikes, others just seemed to be shapes and patterns. Tripods and cameras were stacked high in one corner.

'We've called you to this meeting, Melvin, because we're sure of you now.'

'What do you mean – "sure of me now"?'

'Sure that you're on our side . . .' Bunny's tone was serious.

Melvin felt out of his depth. He wasn't used to being on anyone's side. People who stuck to Perkins' First Law of Survival (Keep Your Head Down) didn't take sides.

'. . . In the fight against the might of Whoppa-Shoppa UK.'

'What?'

Bunny raised his hand. 'First let me explain a few things, Melvin. We've had our doubts about WhoppaShoppa UK ever since they announced their proposed development. I checked out the companies' register on the Business Studies database at College. WhoppaShoppa UK had no other listed retail outlets . . .'

'He means shops,' said Cassandra.

'But you were the only WhoppaShoppa supporter in the class debate!' blurted out Melvin, accusingly.

'Cover,' said Cassandra, 'so as not to arouse suspicion. Anyway, I enjoy getting up people's noses.'

Melvin couldn't argue with that.

'So, who were WhoppaShoppa and what exactly did they want? At first it was just a bit of fun: we weren't that bothered really, because your mum had got the SSNOTS campaign going, our mum had the Town Council behind her, Sarah's mum had the anti-road lobby in her pocket and Pravi's dad was mobilising opposition from the local High Street shops . . .' Bunny broke off and shook his hand in a gesture of disbelief.

'Then,' said Hannah quietly, 'came Monday's meeting at the school. Something had happened there to change our parents' minds, something sinister.'

'You've noticed Mum's eyes too then?' Melvin found himself asking Hannah.

'Of course I have, stupid, do you think I'm blind?'

'Children, please! This is serious!' said Pravi. He meant it.

'Thank you, Pravi,' said Bunny, and took another deep breath. 'Hannah rang me late Monday night in a terrible state – mind you we were pretty wretched after seeing Mum, eh, Cas?'

Cas nodded. 'I couldn't sleep.'

'What about your dad?'

'He's away all week in Wales. On a business conference.'

'Next day we saw all the SSNOTS posters were down. I arranged for Cas to ring me at lunch time at College if she had any information about what was going on. She did: everyone in your class kept mentioning that their parents had seen a video at the meeting. I remembered the new studio up at Hogman's Thorn House. And then I asked around some of my tutors . . . about ways film and video can be used for brain-washing purposes. That's when Matt Graham, who teaches us Film History, told me about subliminal imaging.'

'Sub what?'

'If you stop interrupting, he'll explain,' snapped Hannah.

'In the nineteen thirties, ice cream manufacturers used to pay to have single frame pictures of delicious ice creams inserted into the film reel – just before the interval. The cinema audience would see the frame, but it would flash past their eyes so quickly, they wouldn't *know* they'd seen it. The result was always the same, though. At the interval, the cinema aisles would be choked with people scrambling to get to the ice cream vendor – even if the cinema was freezing and it was snowing outside and ice cream was the last thing people really wanted.'

'Do they still do it now?' asked Melvin. 'It could explain why people buy pot noodles.'

'Bunny's serious,' growled Pravi.

'So am I,' replied Melvin, quickly; still feeling the outsider in this group.

'Subliminal advertising was eventually made illegal,' said Bunny, 'but it still *works*, of course.'

'And you thought – think – this is the technique the WhoppaShoppa people have been using?' Melvin asked Bunny.

'Yes. And – chilling thought – with video and modern digital technology, you can make it work even more effectively. There have been plenty of reports that it's been regularly used by secret service organisations – you know, the CIA and all that. They programme people to do whatever they want. They nickname the people they've programmed . . .'

'Deadheads,' whispered Melvin.

'Oh.' Bunny looked a bit crestfallen. 'You know all about it?'

'Er . . . not really. No . . . er . . . there was this documentary on the telly once,' he stuttered. Nobody believed him, he knew. He was a dreadful liar.

'Mind you, you'd need to be a bit of a brainbox to carry it through, though.'

114

Or empowered by evil, thought Melvin.

'That lifts suspicion from Melvin then,' said Cassandra.

'Mind you,' said Bunny, 'at that stage, we had no evidence. It was only my guesswork.'

'That's where you come in, Melvin,' said Sarah. She had been so quiet that Melvin had quite forgotten she was there.

'Me?'

'Yeah,' Cassandra continued. 'You were acting really weird – answering me back, picking a fight with Pravi.'

'That's because I was upset and frightened too!' Melvin exploded. 'It's rich, isn't it? Other kids have bundles in the playground every day of the week. I lose my temper just once and people treat me as if I was a serial killer or something!'

'Melvin! Listen!' said Hannah.

'Why should I?'

'Because you might learn something.'

Melvin pouted; but listened.

'I followed Pravi and you after school . . .'

'What! You mean when I came here for my bike?' Cassandra nodded.

'I thought I saw someone . . .'

'When you two split up outside the library, I cornered Pravi. He said he suspected you knew more about the WhoppaShoppa business than you were letting on; that you might even be involved . . .'

115

'Thanks, *pal*!'

Pravi looked sheepish.

'I went up to Hogman's Thorn House with Bunny's camcorder, but it was all locked up. Anyway, Pravi came round here later that evening and told us what you'd told him about seeing the security guard from the studios setting up video equipment for the SSNOTS meeting.'

'So we had the connection between Whoppa-Shoppa and the studios confirmed,' said Bunny.

'Then I told them about your theory about the video screens on the WhoppaShoppa centre model at the exhibition,' said Pravi.

'Sharp thinking,' said Bunny – and he meant it. 'But it scares me, Melvin. Scares me rigid. It means that these people are using advanced subliminal imaging techniques for something even more sinister than acquiring a couple of meadows to build a shopping mall on.'

Nobody said anything for a bit.

'If these advanced subliminal imaging techniques are so wonderful,' asked Melvin eventually, 'why do they need to show another video at another meeting on Monday night?'

'Even the most advanced subliminal imaging technique will wear off eventually,' explained Bunny. 'It gets submerged by the mass of other information the brain's receiving all the time. The WhoppaShoppa chief man is obviously taking no risks. It's *possible* our parents will be deadheads right up till the time WhoppaShoppa are able to get their hands on Hogman's Meadow and move the bulldozers in, but just in case anybody begins to come round . . . Monday night's video will make doubly sure.'

'But we can't do anything about it. We can't stop them showing another video, let alone stop our mums and dads falling under the control of WhoppaShoppa UK!' said Melvin. 'Even if we could prevent Monday night's meeting from taking place – burn the school down or whatever, the effects of deadheading might still linger on long enough for the WhoppaShoppa to be built – with all its dead-heading video screens.'

'Something's needed to cancel out the effects of subliminal imaging from our parents' minds quickly and dramatically,' said Bunny. 'It needs to be cinematic images that will associate WhoppaShoppa with something so terrible, so horrifying, so *haunting*, the original effect will be wiped out from their minds.'

'Such as?' Melvin couldn't help the tone of sarcasm from creeping into his voice.

'Pictures of your face?' suggested Cassandra with a sly grin.

'Cas! Please!' Bunny said, annoyed at being interrupted. 'Such as – ' He paused for effect. 'A spectral hound.'

'A what?'

'Forget video nasties. It's the most terrifying film footage I have ever seen,' replied Bunny.

'Shot by a most remarkable cameraman,' added Cassandra, with a strange smile.

'Who?'

'You.'

'Me?'

'Yes. When you took my camcorder from me, you kept your finger on the trigger.'

'Result?' asked Bunny. 'Ten precious close-up seconds of film of a crazed Dobermann leaping at the camera. Put through the College studio's editing suite, that image can be repeated and repeated and repeated.'

'And this is what we show them Monday night?'

Everyone nodded.

'With a matching soundtrack of howls and screams played through the hall speaker system.'

'Will it work?'

'I don't know,' said Bunny sombrely. 'But it's the best chance – the only chance – we've got. The question is, can we get it set up? It'll need someone in the school hall as soon as the WhoppaShoppa people have finished their setting up.'

'That was about four-thirty, last time,' said Pravi.

'Right. And that person will need to stay hidden behind the stage right through to the time the meeting starts. Any volunteers?'

'Can't you do it?' asked Melvin.

'Not me I'm afraid,' shrugged Bunny. 'I'm at College until five. Anyway, if anyone saw me in Norman Burke, they'd lynch me on the spot.' When he'd been a pupil at Norman Burke, he'd been a P.W.S.T. too – and the older teachers all remembered him vividly.

'Same here. If I'm seen about after school, teachers seem to think I'm up to no good, for some reason,' said Cassandra. 'Not that I'll be at school on Monday, on account of my leg.' She winced dramatically and pointed to the bandage wrapped round her ankle.

'Hannah?' asked Bunny.

'I've got to look after Ellie.'

'Sarah?'

'If I'm not back from school by half four, my mum dials 999.'

It sounded daft, but Melvin knew that ever since her little brother had been killed in the accident, what Sarah said was true.

'I've got cricket practice,' said Pravi. 'If I'm missing, the Gibbon will come searching for me. Then I've got to get back to help Mum in the shop.'

Nice one, Pravi, thought Melvin, his heart growing heavier by the second.

'Melvin? It seems to be all down to you.'

Melvin groaned.

'I'll cover for you with Mum,' said Hannah.

'You can say you're having tea at our place,' suggested Pravi.

'How kind,' said Melvin sarcastically.

'Can we really trust him, though?' asked Cassandra with a patronising stare.

That really riled Melvin. 'You'll just have to, won't you!'

'Good,' said Bunny, quickly. 'That's settled then. Now let me explain exactly what you've got to do . . .'

XIII

For the second Monday in succession, Esther's ginger moustache bristles with excitement. The summer term is continuing to go well. WhoppaShoppa UK has hired the school hall for yet another public meeting. They are good customers. Unlike the Pensioners' Bingo Club, they don't leave the hall covered in boiled sweet wrappers. Unlike the Youth Club discos, they don't induce the neighbours to complain about the noise. Unlike the Adult Education Fight-That-Flab Class, they don't leave the school hall smelling of armpits. He glances towards the stage at the wide-screen television monitor dwarfing the table and chair on the stage. He turns to his companion.

'That is a splendid piece of equipment you have there, Mr Summerskill.'

'The very latest Japanese model.'

The two men make their way out of the hall through the rows of empty chairs.

Esther closes the double doors behind them, then looks up and sees a boy, standing transfixed at the end of the corridor like a rabbit caught in the glare of headlamps.

'Hey you! Yes . . .!'

121

13

'That . . . was some haunting!'

'. . . You!'

Esther! That was all Melvin needed. What was *he* doing in school over an hour after the bell had gone? And who was that with him? The twisted leer on the man's face left Melvin in no doubt: this was the Chief Executive of WhoppaShoppa UK, the man empowered by evil to turn everyone in Smallham into deadheads, the man whose dog had almost killed the Washbone, the man his mum called 'Harry Summerskill, a very nice man'.

Everything *had* been going well. Melvin had hidden in the toilets after school. He'd stood splay-legged on the pan and peered through the half-open window at the Psycho and his dog leaving in the white van. He had thought then, that the coast was clear.

'Melvin Perkins!'

'Yes, sir.'

'What are you doing with that bag?'

Think, Perkins! It's easy when you know how, like Cassandra Washbone P.W.S.T., but of course, Melvin didn't know how; he wasn't used to being on the spot like this, staring up into Esther's hairy nostrils, while his beady stare bored a hole in your head.

THINK, PERKINS! When you don't know how, your first thought is usually the same one as when you do: blame someone else.

'Er . . . it's Pravikumar's, sir.'

'And where is Pravikumar?'

'Er . . . cricket practice, sir.' Melvin's confidence was growing. 'I'm taking his bag to the changing rooms.'

The scales fell from Esther's eyes. 'Ah! You've made it up after your little bout of sparring the other day?'

It took a few seconds for Melvin – bright though he was – to realise that Esther was talking about his fight with Pravi.

'Oh yes, sir. That's why I'm taking him his bag. As a favour. To show we've made it up.'

Esther beamed. 'So you shook hands and said you were sorry – like I advised you to?'

He's showing off! thought Melvin. He's showing off to that snake of a man! Give him a hand, Perkins!

'Oh yes, sir. Of course, sir.'

'Melvin, taking a short cut across the school hall is against the rules, is it not?'

You should know, you old fool, thought Melvin, you write them.

'Sorry, sir.'

'Never mind! Because you took my advice, I am inclined to be tolerant on this occasion,' replied Esther. 'Carry on, across the hall – just this once mind!'

And off he strode towards the front entrance with the Chief Executive of WhoppaShoppa.

'You see, Mr Summerskill, what the children of today really need is to be set a firm example.'

'That, and a good thrashing to teach them some respect,' growled the Chief Executive of Whoppa-Shoppa UK.

Behind the stage curtain, Melvin opened his bag. It didn't contain anything belonging to Pravi – other than a copy of *The Giant Vole of Gordian*. What it did contain was a small VCR, a couple of leads and a plug.

Melvin worked quietly and efficiently. He placed the VCR immediately behind the WhoppaShoppa equipment. Then he pulled the connecting lead from the giant wide-screen and inserted Bunny's plug. This had two sockets: one for the Whoppa-Shoppa video and one for his. He plugged both machines in. Then he connected the VCR to the mains socket at the back of the stage. And that was it; all done.

But that, as Bunny had explained, was the easy part.

Melvin crept under the stack of dining tables at the back of the stage. He was completely hidden from the hall proper by the front of stage curtain. It was so quiet! Melvin had never experienced silence in Sir Norman Burke Middle School before and he found it strangely reassuring.

He delved deep into his bag and found the food that the others had given him at school. Two packets of crisps and a can of Coke from Pravi; a slice of chocolate cake from Sarah and half a banana from Cassandra. He took what he thought was about an hour to eat it, but when he finished and looked at his watch, he found that only twenty minutes had gone by. Still two and a half hours before the meeting and the most vital part of his job. He delved deeper into his bag and pulled out Pravi's *The Giant Vole of Gordian*. He flattened its rather battered corners, then opened it at page one:

Murphin the Grule, sage of the Brummis, peered deep into his crystal goblet. 'Beware the tribe of Gordian Voles . . . '

. . . Fangryld, Lord of the Tribe of Gordian Voles sank slowly into the Great Mire of Starq Kraven Mud. A few bubbles broke the dank surface; then it was still. The most evil creature of the Region of Nether Earth was gone forever. THE END.

Melvin closed the book and slipped it back into his bag. The excited buzz of chatter in the hall was growing louder by the second and so was the beating of his heart. Melvin peered out between the metal legs of his nest of dining tables. Each time the doors opened at the back of the hall, the stage curtains fluttered in the draught. Suddenly the gathering hushed. Melvin heard a firm, heavy pair of footsteps striding up the hall. The stage curtains fluttered some more as the footsteps ascended the stage. They stopped.

'Ladies, gentlemen, friends.' Harry Summerskill had a voice that sang. It was confident, insistent, beguiling. 'Welcome . . .'

Now came the difficult, dangerous part.

Melvin crept up to where he'd placed his VCR immediately behind the wide-screen. He was but a metre and a half from Harry Summerskill's feet.

Now he had to wait for the right time.

'WhoppaShoppa's what we need,' intoned Harry Summerskill.

Melvin swore he heard a faint mumbled chorus of 'WhoppaShoppa's what we need.'

'And this video will show us why,' said Harry Summerskill. There was a swish as the hall curtains were drawn to shut out the glow of the summer evening sun. Not that you need a darkened room to watch a video, unless of course, you intend to deadhead the audience by showing them subliminal images.

Melvin heard the sound of a click as a video was inserted into the VCR. A waft of lilting pan pipes filled the school hall and then Harry Summerskill's rich tones sang out:

WhoppaShopping is relaxing,
WhoppaShopping's fun to do,
WhoppaShopping makes you free,
WhoppaShopping is for you . . .

When we're cold or lonely,
When we've mouths to feed,
When we're looking for some fun,
WhoppaShoppa's what we need . . .

The right time was now!

Melvin pressed the PLAYBACK button on Bunny's VCR. Then pushing his hand through the curtains he pulled the connecting plug from the WhoppaShoppa VCR.

At once Cassandra's terrified screams rattled the giant speakers hanging in each corner of the hall.

'*Aaargh! Aargh!*'

The audience looked up, startled. The grisly sound of panting hound; then a triumphant, horrific howl.

On the giant wide-screen, a picture of the new WhoppaShoppa, which Bunny had taken from the model in the library was suddenly filled with the ghostly image of a gigantic slavering Dobermann pinscher baying for blood. Without warning, it seemed to dive through the happy faces on the screen towards the petrified members of the audience.

'Aaargh! Aargh!' This time the screams came from the hall.

Behind the stage. Melvin closed his eyes in silent thanks: it was working.

'Friends! Friends!' Harry Summerskill's desperate, yet already faltering voice had no chance of raising itself above the screaming, yelling audience, or indeed the terrified screaming and terrifying howling from the speaker system as the piece of tape was played again and again and again.

Another howl. This time behind him. This time for real! Melvin swung round to look into the wild, bolting eyes of a Dobermann pinscher.

'It's you, innit?' The sour face of Psycho broke out into a sickening grin. He held the dog on a leash, but all the time was giving it more rein.

'I got you before. Now the dog's going to do you proper this time.'

'Er . . . WhoppaShoppa's what we need,' intoned Melvin.

Psycho stopped for a second; quite taken aback. 'Yeah . . . yeah. WhoppaShoppa's what we need. WhoppaShoppa's what we need . . .'

A second was all Melvin needed to dart round the edge of the curtains and into the darkened hall. The dog strained on the leash; Psycho, caught off guard, stumbled and let go of the dog. It sprang past a terrified Melvin, straight off the stage and into the hall.

Panic, Pandemonium. Screams. Curses. Chairs, kicked over by hurrying feet, skidded along the floor. Curtains tugged at frantically, to let in the summer evening sun. Grown people fighting to push their way through the double doors.

Melvin stood at the edge of the stage and blinked; unable to think straight any more, let alone act.

The dog was all eyes, ears, nose and slavering jaw. Then it scented what it wanted. Harry Summerskill was having trouble collecting up his equipment with his bandaged arm.

'Argh!' He stepped back, pinned by the growling dog against the fire doors that led onto the playground.

'Get it away!' he screamed as Psycho came crawling off the stage.

'Good dog, good boy!' intoned Psycho dumbly. He slipped the leash on the great brute, stroking it between the ears all the time.

'Mr Summerskill! A word!' A voice with the resonance of a foghorn boomed out above the mêlée. Councillor Mrs Washbone was a deadhead no more.

'The people of Smallham will never, never allow this proposed development to take place!' Melvin's mum beat the air with her fist. Neither was she.

Gradually, the people who were left in the hall focused their eyes on Harry Summerskill and made their way, slowly, silently towards him.

'Get back! Or I'll set the dog onto you!' he threatened. It was an idle threat. The dog was interested only in the man who had kicked it the previous evening.

With a sudden thump, Harry Summerskill shoved the fire door bar with his elbow. The doors flew open and he turned and ran. The dog bounded after him and Psycho, its leash wrapped round his wrist, had no option but to follow.

Melvin's arm was being hugged. 'We did it, Melvin!'

'No, Cassandra, *I* did it,' replied Melvin firmly.

'I was out in the audience, helping the screaming and the panic along!'

'I thought you said you couldn't possibly be seen in school!'

'I couldn't . . . not just after school, when you had to set things up. But I was with my mum this evening. Hey, it's a good job you managed it all right or else *I* could've ended up a deadhead too!'

'Let him go!' Councillor Mrs Washbone was saying, as they watched Harry Summerskill hot foot it across the playing fields towards the teachers' car park, closely followed by dog and Gary. 'I think Smallham has seen the last of WhoppaShoppa UK!'

'Here, here!' cried Melvin's mum. 'I hereby convene positively the very last ever meeting of SSNOTS!'

'Come on,' said Cassandra, jumping up onto the stage, 'let's get out of here, before your mum spots you and starts asking questions.' She hobbled up onto the stage, quickly followed by Melvin.

'Well done, Melvin!' said Bunny.

'I suppose you were in the audience too?' asked Melvin.

'Yes. Just got back from College in time.' He rolled up the last length of cable and put it in Melvin's bag. 'Er . . . Melvin . . .?'

'What?'

'I've got another favour to ask.'

'Oh yeah?'

'If you've finished with *The Giant Vole of Gordian*, would you mind if I borrowed it?'

The three of them didn't say much to each other as they walked down Smallham High Street. The late evening sky glowed a warm red as the sun prepared to set over Hogman's Thorn. People drifted into 'The Fuller's Arms' and 'The Railway Tavern' as if it was just another ordinary Monday night in Smallham. Melvin knew, though, that word of the evening's events would soon be around quicker than you could say WhoppaShoppa.

'See ya then,' he said to Bunny and Cassandra as they passed the end of their road.

'Why, where are you going?' asked Bunny with a grin.

'Back to my house.'

'So are we!'

'But . . .'

'Hannah's orders,' shrugged Bunny. 'And you know Hannah's orders. They are not to be lightly disobeyed.

Pravi and Sarah joined them later; Sarah having left her babysitter, Old Mrs Edney, asleep in an armchair. Hannah brought in a tray loaded with Cokes and a huge fresh cream chocolate gateau from the kitchen, more to impress Bunny than anything, Melvin knew.

They toasted each other in Coke. Then they all toasted Bunny for his great job in putting the video together.

'That,' said Bunny, 'was some haunting. Thanks for making it work, Melvin. You deserve a medal.'

As they hadn't got a medal to give to Melvin, they all toasted him in Coke instead.

'Melvin,' asked Cas. 'How *did* you get that dog off me like that?'

'Er . . . it wasn't *me* exactly, Cas,' giggled Melvin.

'Then who was it?'

'It was his friend the ghost!' blurted out Pravi, laughing merrily.

'Oh. Right,' said Cas. She wasn't laughing.

The others had gone by the time Melvin and Hannah's mum came in. She was radiant, with those lively, inquisitive eyes Melvin knew of old.

'Well done, Mum!' said Hannah, with a wink at Melvin.

'Yeah, well done,' said Melvin.

'Melvin?' his mum was looking at him hard. 'Where is our SSNOTS poster?'

'Mum?'

'It's not in the window. I wanted to keep it as a souvenir.'

'I haven't taken it, Mum!'

'Well somebody has. And I got the impression you were never very keen on SSNOTS, Melvin. Probably a secret WhoppaShoppa fan at heart ...'

'Mum!'

Well, you know what parents are like, always jumping unfairly to the wrong conclusions.

'Anyway. Let's celebrate!' Melvin and Hannah's mum was poking about at the back of the fridge. 'I bought a huge fresh cream chocolate cake today. On impulse ...'

Melvin just had time to catch Hannah's horrified look and wipe his mouth instinctively, before their mum turned to them.

'Hannah ...? Melvin ...?'

'Er ... Yes, Mum ...?'

It *was* good to have their mum back from being a deadhead but ...'

'You pair of vultures! Where's my cake?'

133

Neither Melvin's mum, Cas's mum, Sarah Jupe's mum nor Pravi's dad remembered their time as deadheads. It was as if that period of their lives was a gap that had just closed over. The *Smallham Gazette* carried a banner headline: '*SSNOTS TRIUMPH OVER WHOPPASHOPPA BIG BOYS!*'

It was over a fortnight after the SSNOTS triumph that Melvin dared to head in the direction of Hogman's Thorn House again. When he reached HO HO HO, he saw the For Sale sign tied to the gates. He felt strange retracing his movements of a few weeks before, knowing now that he was perfectly safe.

No sooner had he dropped into the grounds, than a voice behind him said, 'Where the blazes have you been, Perkins?'

'Hi, Arnold!'

'Have you no idea how I have fretted about your fate?'

Melvin told him about the spectral haunting, the demise of WhoppaShoppa UK, the end of the deadheads and the For Sale sign on the gates.

'If they have sold the house, it would appear to be the end of the matter,' said Arnold. 'For it was here that they were empowered. It was from here that they drew their knowledge and their strength of purpose.'

'Thanks for coming to the rescue that night we were trapped in here with the dog,' said Melvin.

'Have they taken the girl to jail?' asked Arnold.

'Jail?' The penny dropped and Melvin was obliged to explain to Arnold the difference between a camcorder and a rifle. This took some time, Arnold being a Victorian and all that.

Melvin sat and leant back against the wall. The gardens of HO HO HO were certainly a peaceful spot. The trees rustled untroubled above his head. That, and the occasional birdsong, was the only sound to be heard.

'You will still visit me, won't you,' asked Arnold quietly, 'even though the house is being sold?'

'Of course,' said Melvin; and he meant it. He had braved mad dogs and psychopathic security guards to visit his ghost friend; any other difficulties the new owners might present would be mere peanuts.

'Good. Because you are my only hope.'

'Hope?'

'For avenging my murder!'

'Arnold, I've said before, I can't see how . . .'

'It has to be done! I cannot bear to have to haunt this small space on earth for all eternity!' Arnold paused. 'Much as I enjoy your company, Perkins.'

Melvin shook his head, despairingly.

'You are empowered, Perkins. There must be a reason why you were given strength and fortitude by the spirit of this place . . .'

'Of course there is! It was to turn my mum back from being a deadhead!'

Arnold paused. 'There *must* be a reason too, Perkins, why you, and you only, have been empowered to see me.'

Later, as he freewheeled his way down Hogman's Hill, Arnold's words went round and round in Melvin's mind. Perhaps he was right. Perhaps the task of avenging Arnold's murderers *had* been given to him. So much for Perkins' First Law of Survival.

Avenging a murdered ghost? It did seem an impossible problem. Still at least, thought Melvin, I can apply myself single-mindedly to it, now that everything is back to normal in Smallham.

Now that the danger of people being turned into deadheads is no more.

XIV

There are four of them. Three men and a woman.
They sit around the gnarled table in the farmhouse
kitchen, stony-faced.

'I put the house on the market today,' the woman
says.

'Angela! You had no right without consulting Guy,
Darius or me!'

'I agreed to it,' says Darius.

'So did I,' says Guy.

'So why wasn't I approached?'

'After the mess you've made of things, Harry?'

'We need the house! How else are we empowered
with the strength and the knowledge to carry the
deadheading programme through?'

'I have made plans to buy it back, under another
name, of course,' says Angela, with icy calm.

'Little good the house did you or the programme!'
mutters Darius, glowering darkly at Harry.

'If you think you can do better, why don't you
take control of the future programming attempts?'
snaps Harry.

'I will!' declares Darius. 'If Angela and Guy are
agreed.'

They nod their assent.

'I can't believe a mere kid could've fouled up!' sighs Harry, visibly shaking with anger and frustration.

'I can,' says Guy. 'I see enough of them every day of my working life to believe they are capable of anything.'

Darius coughs, discreetly.

'That's why, I believe we should forget the adults next time.'

The others register the ice-cold smile on his face.

'That's why I believe we must deadhead the kids, instead. Every one of them.'

and the DEADHEADS

2

The Genius Academy

When Cassandra Washbone, the tone-deaf school troublemaker, announces that she's going to become an opera singer, Melvin is appalled. Such an awful idea can mean only one thing: the Deadheads are back. Fate intervenes when Melvin accidentally wins the local children's art competition and finds himself at the mercy of the sinister wonder-worker, Darius O'Fee.

What is the secret behind the mysterious Genius Academy? Melvin must find out before he, Cassandra and all of their friends are turned into Deadheads…

This is the second in a series of four gripping thrillers chronicling Melvin Perkins' battle against the Deadheads.